FINALLY FELL

ELENA AITKEN

Also by Elena Aitken

The Springs Series

Summer of Change

Falling Into Forever

Second Glances

Winter's Burn

Midnight Springs

She's Making A List

Summit of Desire

Summit of Seduction

Summit of Passion

Fighting For Forever

The Springs Collection: Volume 1

The Springs Collection: Volume 2

The Springs Collection: Volume 3

The Springs Complete Collection - Books 1-10

The McCormicks

Love in the Moment

Only for a Moment

One more Moment

In this Moment

From this Moment

Our Perfect Moment

Stand Alone Stories

All We Never Knew

Drawing Free

Sugar Crash

Composing Myself

Betty & Veronica

The Escape Collection

Vegas

Nothing Stays in Vegas

Return to Vegas

Timber Creek

When We Left

When We Were Us

When We Began

When We Fell

Timber Creek: The Complete Series

Castle Mountain Lodge

Unexpected Gifts

Hidden Gifts

Unexpected Endings - Short Story

Mistaken Gifts

Secret Gifts

Goodbye Gifts

Tempting Gifts

Holiday Gifts

Promised Gifts

Accidental Gifts

The Castle Mountain Lodge Collection: Books 1-3

The Castle Mountain Lodge Collection: Books 4-6

Chapter One

THE LADIES' room was a welcome reprieve. The moment I stepped through the doors and they closed behind me, dulling the din of the constant conversation and background music, both of which seemed to be louder than usual, I felt like I could breathe again.

Mercifully, the restroom seemed to be empty. The only thing worse than making small talk with a never-ending flow of colleagues and clients was doing it in the washroom. Despite myself, I chuckled at the thought of discussing the latest financials with the CEO of MultiTech, the company I was currently the chief financial officer of, while we touched up our makeup. Especially considering the CEO was Shane Grant, a rather large, bearded man.

In fact, most of my colleagues were men. Escaping to the ladies' room alone was a definite perk of being one of the only women in a high-powered executive role. I'd worked hard to be in the position I was in. A few minutes of respite from these events shouldn't be too much of an ask.

Shouldn't be.

I inhaled deeply and tried to shake the melancholy hanging

over me. I usually loved these events. I'd dedicated my life to my career and not one time had it been a hardship. While my best friends were getting married, I was working late into the night, choosing the hardest accounts to prove myself. When they were having babies and going to Mommy and Me classes, I was wining and dining clients, fending off inappropriate advances and proving myself a loyal and indispensable asset to the business by working sixty-hour workweeks. When they were buying houses and hosting dinner parties, I was living off takeout while I worked by the dim glow of my computer screen well past midnight.

And I loved it.

Never once had I felt like I'd missed out.

Not one time did I wish I'd chosen a different path in life.

I thrived on the challenge of my career. Working the numbers, finding opportunities to grow a company through the bottom line. It was exhilarating.

And these black-tie nights were all part of it.

I used to live for this shit. Schmoozing potential clients, or merger opportunities, was my jam. And I was good at it. Stuffy corporate types never saw me coming. They saw a tall, good-looking blonde with red lipstick, and instantly their guard fell. Those were the easy ones. The ones who thought with their dick first. The ones who didn't even consider that a pretty girl could possibly have the brains to know a thing or two about money, let alone how it could be used to the ultimate advantage.

And then there were men like Shane Grant, my boss. He was one of the good ones. He not only recognized how smart I was, but how advantageous I could be for him in his tech company. The thing that people didn't know about tech companies was that innovation was only a small part of the job. The bigger job was buying up the constant flow of start-ups that popped up and threatened your business.

And that's where I came in.

Not only could I boil down the numbers into a bottom line that would benefit everyone, nobody expected it from me. It only took me a few minutes of conversation with a potential acquisition target to know what I needed to know. It was amazing what men would say after a few minutes of flirting with a pretty woman. More often than not, before the first drink was done, I knew about their cash flow—usually their lack of it—their bottom line, and exactly how much—or how little—it would take to buy them up.

I was damn good at my job.

But more and more lately, it was starting to feel empty. The heady rush that used to fuel me was slowly being replaced with disappointment. It's not that it wasn't challenging anymore. It was. That was the thing about working with numbers and people. There was always a challenge to sink my teeth into.

Still…I couldn't help feeling that there was more to life. It was troubling that I'd been feeling that way more often lately. Especially because I didn't know what *more* meant.

With a sigh, I examined my reflection. I'd been gone long enough. I would need to get back out there before my presence was missed. Despite the fact that my bright-red lipstick was still perfectly applied, I pulled the tube from my clutch and carefully reapplied a coat. My long blonde hair had been pulled up into a tight twist at the back of my head, leaving my neck bare. The dress I'd chosen was black and elegant. Cut deep enough in the front to be sexy, but not slutty. Just enough to catch the eye. It was long-sleeved, but off the shoulder with a low back. It was more skin than I usually exposed at a work function, but I didn't care. The dress looked amazing. And I felt fabulous in it.

There was a mid-thigh slit in the long skirt that offered glimpses of my lean legs that I knew looked impressive with the red stilettos I'd chosen to match my signature lipstick.

I capped the lipstick and returned it to my purse as the door of the restroom opened with a wave of noise. A giggling redhead who'd clearly had one too many drinks for a work function all but fell into the room before the door shut behind her.

"Oh, I didn't—hi," the girl said as she noticed me for the first time. She straightened up and made her way to the sink. "I didn't realize there was anyone in here."

I shrugged a little, not remotely interested in starting a conversation. If I was going to be subjected to small talk, I wasn't going to be doing it in the bathroom with someone's drunk date.

I turned to leave.

"Sorry," the girl said, stopping me. "Would you mind…"

I turned to see her shimmying her body awkwardly as she reached up behind her back.

"This zipper…it's…"

"Sure." I put my clutch on the counter and rescued the girl from her skintight dress by working the zipper down her back far enough that she could manage the rest. "There you go."

"You're a lifesaver. Thank you." She shuffled to a stall as she wiggled the fabric up around her hips. "I don't know why they make these dresses so impossible." She spoke through the closed door. "I mean, I can hardly sit down, let alone pull it up enough to pee." A giggle filled the air as I moved to leave. "Oh!" she shouted out. "Can you please wait a minute?"

Could she read minds? I froze and stared at the closed door.

"I won't be able to get back into my dress," she continued. "Please."

It's not as if I could say no. "Okay."

"You are a saint." She laughed again, and I heard a flush before she emerged, looking visibly relieved. "Thank you so much." She washed her hands while I waited. "My name is Trista, by the way. This is my first time at one of these," she continued without waiting for a response. "It's so fun, don't you think?""

I didn't. Fun was not a word I'd ever use to describe these functions. Not even when I was Trista's age.

"You look like you've been to one or two before," she continued. "I mean, I'm probably the youngest one here. Don't you think?"

Was she saying I was old?

I swallowed hard and waited for her to turn around so I could zip her up and get out of there. My little break was quickly turning into a reminder that the only thing I hated more than small talk was making it with the bimbo dates that some of the men insisted on bringing to these functions. As if dating a girl who was barely over the legal drinking age was going to make them feel any younger. Hell, maybe it did. But it sure didn't make them look anything but desperate and more than a little ridiculous.

"Nice to meet you, Trista." I gave her a bright smile. "And yes, you are definitely one of the younger women here, but don't let that intimidate you. I was once—"

"Oh, I'm not."

I watched as she reached into her dress and lifted first one of her huge breasts into place in her dress and then the other, before turning to present her back and the zipper to me.

"I mean, I am the prettiest girl in the room. No offense."

I tugged her zipper up sharply, making her gasp.

"None taken."

I was quickly losing my patience with this girl.

"But you have to admit," Trista spun to face the mirror and fluff her hair, "these places are perfect for finding a rich guy, right? I mean, all it takes is a quick blow job in the car on the way home and they're in love, am I right?" She wiggled her eyebrows. "You look like you know exactly what I mean."

I did?

"Oh, definitely." I nodded. "If you'll excuse me, Trista. I should get back."

"Of course." She pursed her lips together seriously. "You can't keep them waiting. These guys need so much attention."

It was an effort not to roll my eyes as I left her primping her ridiculously young, firm body and rejoined the party. The thing was, Trista wasn't wrong. The majority of the men at these events were either on their second, third, or fourth wife—each younger than the last—or they were there with a girl like Trista.

It was a gross overgeneralization, of course, and there were exceptions. But I couldn't help but think that those exceptions were getting harder and harder to find. Not that I was looking.

I wasn't.

The only man I needed in my life was one to scratch the occasional itch before getting out of my bed and back to his own apartment before the sun came up. Period.

"Brittany! Just the woman I was looking for."

I turned, my smile perfectly in place, to greet my boss, Shane Grant, who also happened to be my best friend Jessie's new boyfriend. It was a long story, but they were perfect for each other. Making Shane Grant one of those very rare exceptions I was just thinking about.

"Shane." I leaned in as he greeted me with a kiss on the cheek. "Jessie." I pulled my friend in for a hug. I knew she'd feel a little out of place at the club, but I loved that she was here. "You look amazing."

She really did. Ever since she'd sold her diner and fallen completely into her new relationship with Shane, she was like a totally different woman. She deserved it, too.

"Thank you." Jessie twirled a little in her dress. "But seriously, Britt. You look amazing."

Shane put his arm around Jessie's waist and pulled her close. "I'm a little partial," he said as he kissed her on the cheek. "But Jessie really does look incredible." He flashed a smile at me. "Brittany, you look exceptional as always."

I laughed. "Thanks, Shane. It's been a good night. I had an interesting conversation with Chad Duvall. I think he'll be open to a meeting next week." I spent the next few minutes filling him in on my conversations so far before his attention was distracted.

"Sorry, Brittany," he said as he waved at someone behind me. "But I have to change the subject quickly." He looked to Jessie again. "I know a lot went down between you," he said to her. "And I know you've had the chance to clear the air, but it's important to me that you two get to know each other as friends. And Brittany, even though he's been sharing our office space, I don't think you've properly met him either."

I didn't have to turn around to see who Shane was talking about. My spine stiffened, and at the same time, my stomach flipped. I'd only actually met him once, when he rectified his terrible behavior in acquiring Jessie's diner. We'd hardly even spoken to each other at that meeting; still, I'd had a very hard time getting his green eyes out of my mind. The way he'd looked at me. No man had ever looked at me that way before, and I couldn't quite put my finger on why it was different. Only that it was. And it made me feel things. A lot of things. Things that had followed me into my dreams. It was true—he was sharing office space with us at MultiTech. It was also true that I'd done my best to avoid him and his unnerving gaze.

But I couldn't ignore him forever. He *was* a good friend of Shane's. Besides, I didn't even know him. And it was probably just a one-time, chance thing that I'd misread.

I put my well-practiced smile in place and slowly turned around as Shane greeted him.

"Trent! Good to see you, man."

But it wasn't a one-time thing. The second I turned around, my eyes locked on Trent Thomas's green gaze and it happened again. The look. Like he could *see* me. Like he *knew* me. Like he *wanted* me. All of me.

My breath hitched in my throat in a way that made it hard to breathe, but I didn't look away. Neither did he. It wasn't until Shane said, "And who is your beautiful date tonight?" that I finally tore my gaze away from Trent's, to see the woman I hadn't noticed until then.

Trista.

Brittany Donahue.

Damn.

Somehow, every time I saw the woman, she looked sexier than the last. Her glacier-blue eyes pierced me, challenging me. But I held her gaze, unwavering, until my date tugged on my arm, at the exact same moment Brittany looked away.

"Hi," the girl next to me whose name I'd momentarily forgotten, cooed. "I'm Trista."

Trista. Right.

She thrust her hand out along with her massive tits and tossed her hair over her shoulder with a giggle as Shane politely took her hand in greeting. She was so obvious, it was embarrassing. Mostly for her. But I couldn't help but cringe.

My gaze moved back to Brittany, who didn't bother to hide her look of disgust at Trista's behavior. As if she sensed me, she looked up and raised an eyebrow in question as if to say, *"Really?"*

In response, I pressed my lips together and shrugged a little before introducing my date to Jessie. "Shane's fiancée." I made a point to emphasize the word, because even though Trista was there with me, she was definitely the type to look for a bigger and better opportunity.

I knew the type. Hell, I knew it well. I'd exclusively dated

Tristas for years: young, giggly, big tits that looked good in a tight dress—and even better in my hands.

Dating Tristas was easy.

She got what she wanted—treated to expensive dinners, drinks and occasional gifts with the opportunity to meet her next sugar daddy—and I got what I wanted—a plus one at these boring events, followed by a hot fuck before going home alone, just the way I liked it.

And it was how I liked it.

Trista, message received, had resumed her rubbing up on my side. Her tits pressed into me, and one hand slid down over my ass.

I cleared my throat and took a small, hopefully subtle, step to the side.

Brittany swallowed a chuckle.

Not so subtle then.

I ignored her and focused on Shane and Jessie. "How are the two of you?" I looked directly at Jessie, who had every reason to hate me after I'd tried to acquire her diner, Rosie's, for a pittance a few months earlier. To be fair, it was only business, and I would have done the exact same thing no matter who it was. Still, when I learned that she was involved with Shane and—more importantly—realized for the first time how *just doing business* could impact real people and real lives, I took a different approach to the acquisitions division of my business. A much more humane approach. So far, not only had it worked, it made me feel like a better person to make fair deals with people instead of trying to get the lowest possible price for my bottom line. It felt good, and I had Jessie to thank for that. Something I'd done repeatedly ever since making amends with her.

Still, her friend Brittany clearly hadn't gotten the memo.

Ice Queen would be a generous description of the woman who stood silently glaring at me next to Jessie, almost as if she were on guard, as the three of us made small talk for a few minutes.

"I'm so sorry," Shane said, changing the subject abruptly. "I wanted to make sure the two of you had been properly introduced." He gestured for Brittany to step forward. She did so, but the mask of indifference on her gorgeous face remained firmly in place.

"We've met." Still, I held my hand out, wanting to touch her. "But it never hurts to have a proper introduction after everything that's transpired." I gave her my most charming smile as I carefully shook Trista off my left side. "It is absolutely my pleasure to officially meet you, Brittany. My good friend Shane here speaks very highly of you."

For a moment, I was certain she was going to snub me altogether. My hand dangled in the space between us, but I was a patient man. I focused my eyes on her, but she didn't quite meet my gaze. I was almost ready to admit defeat when her red lips very deliberately moved into what had to be a carefully practiced smile.

"Trent."

Her voice oozed with social graces. Oh yes, she knew exactly what she was doing. But when her manicured hand finally slipped into mine, her carefully constructed persona faltered.

I saw it, even if no one else noticed when her chest hitched with a sharp intake of breath as my fingers held hers in a soft, but firm grip.

Heat flashed between us, and even I had a hard time not reacting to what should have been an innocent touch.

"It's…" She worked hard to recover without incident. "It's very nice to finally meet you in better circumstances." She held her smile on her face as finally, her eyes met mine. Again, her pupils dilated, making her pale-blue eyes darken.

With lust?

Damn. I couldn't know with certainty that's what she was feeling. But fuck, it was most definitely what I was feeling.

One. Simple. Touch.

As quick as it was there, it was gone. She'd withdrawn her hand, her gaze once more fixed just over my shoulder.

"Aren't you both in the same office?" Jessie asked, oblivious —as was everyone else—as to what had just transpired between us. "How is it you've never run into each other?"

It was an excellent question. One I was pretty sure I already knew the answer to.

"If I didn't know better," I said with just enough mischief in my voice to keep it light, "I'd think that Brittany's been avoiding me."

I saw the flinch. I was right. She *had* been avoiding me. But why?

"Why would I be avoiding you?" Her voice didn't reveal anything. "After all, I don't even know you."

Jessie looked between her friend and back to me.

Out of the corner of my eye, I saw her roll her eyes. So, I wasn't the only one who recognized that something was up with Brittany.

But if Jessie thought her friend was acting strange, there must be some kind of secret friendship pact, because she didn't say anything, but swiftly changed the subject to ask about the development that was going in where her diner had once stood.

Distracted, I did my best not to be rude to her, especially considering we were tentatively building a friendship after our rocky start, and answered all of her questions as Shane and Brittany fell into a separate conversation beside us. Distractedly, I realized Trista had found her way to the bar—again— and the bartender who didn't try to hide the fact that he was ogling her breasts as he poured her stronger than necessary drinks.

I shook my head slightly. I'd peel her away from the bar later; after all, even annoying and vapid, she was still my date. And her tits *were* magnificent.

"So what do you think, Trent?"

I cleared my head and refocused on the conversation, which had clearly shifted again.

Shane watched me, waiting for an answer. "What do you think?"

"Sounds good."

"It does?" Shane raised his eyes.

Shit. It was the wrong answer, apparently. But, I was invested now. "Why not?" I said with confidence.

"Looks like you're outvoted, Shane," Jessie said next to me.

"You're supposed to be on my side, man," Shane said with a groan. But despite the fact that he'd obviously conceded to whatever it was his girlfriend wanted, he didn't look upset.

But I was still confused.

"Do I get a vote?" Brittany asked.

"No way," Jessie jumped in. "You're my friend, so obviously you agree with me."

"Sure," Brittany said with an emphasized smile. "A dinner party sounds like fun, Jessie. I can't wait."

So that's what I'd agreed to. It could be worse. I didn't mind a dinner party among friends. It was definitely better than these stuffy affairs, and even they weren't all bad. There were worse things than being surrounded by gorgeous women. And that was definitely one of the perks of these things. My eyes settled on Brittany, who looked damned good in her black off-the-shoulder dress. It was fitted and clung to her in all the right ways. Her body was long and lean, her breasts smaller than what usually caught my eye, but still beautiful. In fact, everything about Brittany was stunning. Elegant in a way that demanded attention and respect.

"Not a dinner party," Jessie corrected. "A *housewarming* party." She laughed. "Super casual. Just a few friends."

"Tell me when," I said with a smile as Trista reappeared at my side and threaded her arm through mine. "I'll be there."

I heard Shane mutter *traitor*, but he chuckled as he said it. It was no secret that he'd do anything for Jessie. My friend, who'd once been burned so badly by a woman that he'd sworn off any relationship longer than one night, was completely head over heels and one hundred percent devoted to the single mom.

And if it could happen to Shane…

My eyes drifted down to Trista, who looked up at me with hooded lids full of promise. Or too much alcohol. Either way, it was definitely time to take her home. But it wasn't my date who held my attention as I quickly said our goodbyes.

"It was nice to properly meet you, Trent." Brittany's voice gave nothing away, but I was certain I heard the slightest trace of sarcasm there. Her eyes sparkled as she looked in my direction.

I took her hand again, this time squeezing it just a little as the heat flowed between us. "I hope to see you soon, Brittany." I looked straight into her eyes so I didn't miss the flash in them. "Now that I know you're not avoiding me."

Her cheeks pinked. Not enough for anyone else to notice, except me, as she withdrew her hand, clearly flustered.

I turned to leave, Trista still glued to my left side.

"Enjoy the rest of your night."

Brittany's voice reached me and just like that, I knew there was only one way I'd be enjoying the rest of my night. And unfortunately, that wasn't likely to happen.

Chapter Two

IT FELT like forever before I was finally able to make my excuses and leave the club behind. The cool, calm quiet of my penthouse condo welcomed me like a hug the moment I stepped through the door.

My girlfriends all made fun of my style, complaining that they could never be comfortable in my space. Not that I cared. I hadn't decorated for them. I'd decorated for me. And I loved it. The crisp clean lines of the white marble counters, that blended seamlessly with the white tile floors and slightly off-white walls, were soothing. My pale-gray leather couch was much more comfortable than it looked, and it wasn't as if there were no color at all in my space. The artwork had been designed in shades of blues that matched the throw cushions and a few choice hand-blown glass pieces.

Yes, it was simple. Unfussy.

Just like me.

It was home. And as long as I loved it, that's all that mattered.

A sharp meow filled the air the moment I closed the front door behind me.

Okay, it wasn't just me that mattered. It was also Sheldon.

I bent down and gathered my fluffy black and white cat into my arms. Sheldon immediately nuzzled into my neck, his loud purr filling my ears.

"See? I'm not alone," I said to Sheldon.

The girls might think I was lonely, but they were wrong. I had Sheldon. We'd been together for just over ten years, and it was hands down the best relationship I'd ever been in. Not that I'd ever had an actual relationship with a man. But who needed it? The last thing I needed was someone cluttering up my space, complaining that I worked too much, or that I made more money than they did. Men were all the same. Insecure and threatened by a strong woman with her shit together.

I didn't need it.

I scratched Sheldon's head and tried to snuggle him closer, but he had other ideas as he meowed and squirmed to be let down.

Despite his fluffiness, he was definitely not a cuddly cat. I liked his style.

Attention on his own terms. When he wanted it and only as much as he wanted. And then...leave him alone.

It was just like mine, which was why we worked well together.

I shimmied out of my dress and dropped it in the hamper for dry cleaning later.

It was late and I should get some sleep, but I was too keyed up after the party.

No.

After Trent Thomas.

The man got under my skin, and I couldn't quite put my finger on why.

Not true.

I knew exactly what it was.

It was the way he looked at me. No man ever looked at me that way.

Sure, they looked with desire, intimidation, maybe even respect in the middle of a business deal. But Trent looked at me with *interest*. Like he was actively trying to figure me out or learn something about me without asking.

Like he *cared*.

But that was ridiculous. Why would a man like Trent Thomas, who'd hardly ever met me, *care* about me?

It didn't make sense.

Nor did it matter to me. A minor detail I needed to keep reminding myself of.

Regardless, I wasn't going to be able to sleep, so I tugged on a pair of leggings over my long legs and an oversized sweater and followed Sheldon out to the living room. I poured myself a glass of soda water from the bottle in the fridge and contemplated adding a splash of vodka but decided against it.

I hardly ever drank, and that was by design. Alcohol caused you to drop your guard, loosen your inhibitions and make decisions you'd regret. Not that I'd personally experienced it. That was also by design.

But I'd seen enough people have their life changed, both in small and major ways, because of alcohol to know that it was best just to steer clear of it altogether.

My eyes drifted to the large box that had arrived earlier that day. I had the delivery guy put it in the corner, and I had full intentions of leaving it there, well...at least until I could have it moved to the storage unit I had in the parking garage. There was nothing of value in the box. That I knew without even looking inside.

Still, almost against my will, I felt drawn to the box until I stood over it.

Addressed to me, it had been sent by Fraser Lawrence. My late mother's assistant.

And that's how I knew it would hold nothing of value. She'd donated everything she had to charity. Everything.

Mom and I had never been close. She'd been a workaholic up until her death six months ago. The only thing she cared about was her work as a corporate lawyer. I'd held some sort of childlike fantasy that when her assistant called to tell me she was dying, it was because my mother loved and cared about me and wanted nothing more than to have me at her side so she could apologize for not being the mother I needed and deserved.

But I couldn't have been more wrong.

The moment I got the call, I'd dropped everything and caught the next flight to Vancouver, where she'd moved the second I'd graduated from high school. Despite everything that had happened over the years—the missed school functions, the forgotten birthdays, the Christmas cards addressed by her assistant, the complete lack of interest in having me in her life—she was still my mother, and she was the only family I had left. And yes, I was a practical person. Maybe even a little *too* practical, although it was a fine line I walked to keep myself from being as cold as the woman who raised me. Still, I couldn't help but think that her reaching out meant something.

Of course, I'd been disappointed. Again.

She'd been surprised and not entirely pleased to see me in her hospital room. It had been Fraser who'd reached out. Not her. I should have known.

Still, I stayed with her and even held her hand as she took her final breath a few days later.

I never got an apology or an explanation or...it didn't matter anymore.

Just like whatever was in the box didn't matter.

Still...

Before I could talk myself out of it again, I pulled at the

tape on the edge. It gave way easily and tore off, leaving the box open and accessible.

There was a note on top.

I thought you should have these.

~Fraser

Odd. They weren't from my mother at all.

Still, curiosity got the best of me, and I lifted the tissue away to reveal…paintings?

My heart leapt to my throat, making it hard to breathe as I pulled the first canvas from the box. It was a little girl, her back to the artist, her long blonde hair falling down her back, a ratty stuffed cat clutched in her hand as she stared out the window.

It was me.

The next piece was of a young woman; her long hair covered half her face and cast shadows over the other half. Still, there was no mistaking that it was also an image of me in my twenties.

I knew without looking at the signatures in the corner that there was only one person who could have painted them. Still, my eyes searched out the familiar scribble.

P. Donahue.

My father.

I swallowed hard and propped the paintings up against the wall.

Maybe a little vodka wouldn't hurt after all.

No sooner were we in the back seat of the town car than her hands were sliding up my thighs.

Apparently, everyone had tried to leave the party at the same time. Either that, or there was some kind of accident or conspiracy keeping me longer than necessary in the back of the private car with the woman who was making no secret of the fact that she would happily help me pass the time until we got back to her apartment.

"You're so sexy," Trista murmured against my neck as she trailed her long fingernails through my hair. "But you know what would be even sexier?"

I had a pretty good idea as her fingers started to work at the knot in my tie.

She was a good-looking girl, and those tits...they'd been begging to be released from that dress and put into my hands all night. Which had been my entire plan for the evening.

Take Trista to the party.

And then, take her home.

Where I'd not only get those tits in my hands but in my mouth. Her nipples between my lips, sucking and nibbling until she cried out for more.

Hell, earlier when I'd picked her up and seen her plump, pink lips, the only thing I could picture was having them wrapped around my cock all the way home.

Yes, that had definitely been the plan.

Before.

I closed my eyes as Trista began kissing and sucking on my lips again, and it wasn't my date's face that appeared in my imagination. It was Brittany. It was her long blonde hair, released from the tight twist on the back of her head, falling over my face as she kissed me.

It was her bright-red lips wrapped around my cock, her

glacial-blue eyes looking up at me while she sucked me off. My fingers wrapped through the silky strands of her hair while I—

"Trent?"

My eyes snapped open to see Trista, who'd succeeded in loosening my tie and had somehow managed to wiggle her skintight dress up over her hips so she could straddle my lap, watching me. Those huge tits, still encased in her dress, were now directly in my face.

I blinked. "Sorry," I said. "I didn't hear the question."

She giggled, certain I'd been distracted by her. And I should have been. Trista *was* my date. She was here in front of me, ready and willing to do all kinds of dirty things with me with no strings attached. And that's exactly what I wanted. That was exactly why I liked girls like Trista.

Easy. Uncomplicated. Sexy as hell.

Just because Brittany's face had appeared in my imagination momentarily, it was nothing more than a product of the fact I'd just seen her. It didn't mean anything. She was a good-looking woman. And we'd spent time chatting. That was all. It meant nothing.

But I'd spent a lot of time chatting with other good-looking women and never had they taken over my fantasies when I was with another woman. Ever.

Still.

Nothing with Brittany was ever going to happen. But with Trista, I would most certainly get the release I needed. And what was that saying about what's in front of you…

"I asked if you wouldn't mind unzipping my dress." Trista batted her eyelashes and pressed herself down on what was already a throbbing erection in my pants. "It's just so tight," she continued, her voice full of promise. "And it's going to be a long drive."

My eyes glanced to the privacy shade that had already been put in place by the driver. He wasn't new.

I shifted my focus back to my date. "Well, we can't have you being uncomfortable, can we?"

My fingers pulled the zipper down her back before trailing up the smooth skin beneath the fabric. Trista was a beautiful woman, if not a little annoying.

And shallow and young and…

Not at all like Brittany.

I swallowed hard and forced thoughts of the untouchable blonde from my head. She wasn't here. Trista was here, and she was currently sliding her dress off and—

"You're gorgeous." My hands moved instinctively to her breasts the moment she presented them to me.

Trista giggled and lifted her body so her tits were inches from my mouth. I obliged by kissing first one, then the other as Trista's hands found their way to the bulge in my pants. She moved quickly, unbuckling my belt and sliding the leather free. A moment later, she was in my pants, freeing my hard cock.

I tried. I really did. More than anything, my body wanted the release that Trista promised, but my mind could not focus on the woman in front of me. Even as she shimmied down in the seat and lowered her head to my lap, my thoughts went to Brittany.

Had she taken someone home?

No. She hadn't been at the party with anyone, and she wasn't the type to pick up random men. Especially not at a business function.

Trista wrapped her lips around my length and a moan slipped reflexively from my throat.

Did Brittany have a boyfriend? Was there a man in her life who got to have those red lips on his, who got to trace the soft, creamy skin of her neck down between her breasts?

No.

I knew instinctually there was no man in her life.

Still, I couldn't stop thinking about her. The more I tried to stop, the more she dominated my thoughts.

My cock twitched with Trista's attentions, but it wasn't my date who was turning me on.

It was wrong.

"Stop." I grabbed Trista's shoulders and pulled her up and off me.

She sat back, almost completely naked with her dress around her waist, her tits bouncing. Her lipstick was smeared and her mouth made a shocked O as she assessed me. "Was I doing something—"

"I'm just not into it."

She lifted an eyebrow. "You seemed plenty into it to me."

There was no way I was going to make an already shitty and awkward situation even worse by admitting to her that my hard-on had very little to do with her and almost everything to do with a woman who'd hardly given me the time of day.

"I'm not." I finished tucking my still very hard dick back into my pants. "I'll take you home."

Realization slowly dawned on Trista's face as she realized I was rejecting her. "You'll *take me home*? Just like that?"

I nodded curtly and sent a quick text to my driver with the change in plans. No sense in adding to Trista's humiliation by lowering the privacy screen. "Can I help you with your dress?"

She struggled into the skintight garment and reluctantly turned her back to me to help with the zipper considering there was no other choice for it. "Did I do something wrong?" Trista finally asked. "I thought we were having a good time."

"No," I answered honestly. "You didn't do anything wrong." It wasn't her fault that for the first time ever, I wanted something besides a quick fuck in the back seat on the way home with a woman who would be more than happy to oblige and never speak to me again.

No. I wanted something very, very different.

I wanted Brittany.

———

Ultimately, I didn't opt for vodka. But only because it felt wrong to drink alone. Especially because I was sitting on the living room floor, staring at paintings that my alcoholic artist of a father, who'd abandoned me as a child, had painted—of me.

That was just wrong.

Why did my mother have these paintings? Why had I never seen them before? Had she spoken to my father before she died?

So many questions that I'd never have answers to, and it only pissed me off. It shouldn't be a surprise to me anymore. Not after all of these years, and especially not after her death. But still, my mother's complete and total indifference to me or my feelings was startling. Even from beyond the grave, she couldn't throw me a crumb. A little nugget of something that I could hold onto that would let me know that despite how cold she'd been while I was growing up, and how I'd always been made to feel like an inconvenience that was *so much like your father*, that maybe she really did love me under that hard shell.

But of course, she wouldn't. And finally, at the ripe age of forty-one, I was finally starting to accept that maybe she didn't love me. Maybe she *couldn't.* Not the way I wanted her to.

I dropped my head, and Sheldon chose that moment to crawl onto my lap, his soft tail trailing over my face, making it tickle.

"You silly cat." I scooped him up and, despite his meowls of protest, snuggled him close.

I thought I was over all that *mommy* stuff. It had taken a lot of therapy and the unwavering love and support of the family I'd chosen—my girlfriends—to move past it. But I had. *Hadn't I?*

These paintings just opened up more questions. My father

left when I was ten. The first painting made sense. Too much sense. But the second one...how did he know what I looked like well enough to paint it? Where was he? Had he been close? Had he wanted to see me after all? My mother always claimed he'd chosen his art over us.

"Your father isn't capable of loving anything as much as he loves his paintbrushes, Brittany," she said. "Knowing him, he's already so lost in his work that he's forgotten all about us already. It'll do you good to forget about him, too."

I'd been ten. Way too young to understand anything except that the man who tucked me in every night, read me stories, and let me play with his paints and brushes in his studio was gone. But old enough to know not to ask too many questions.

He'd left me a small beat-up wooden box with a few brushes and some tubes of watercolors that I kept hidden under my bed for almost two years before she'd caught me painting a landscape in a sketchpad I'd bought with my allowance. My mother worked late Tuesdays and Thursdays, so I'd rush home from school, finish my homework and paint. I never told anyone. Not even my best friends.

But that Tuesday night, she'd come home early and I'd been so lost in my art that by the time I heard the front door close, it was too late.

"What do you think you're doing?" she'd screamed. She almost never raised her voice. "You're going to be just like him." She tore the sketchbook from me and, while I watched, ripped every single page from the coils. "It's no life, Brittany. It will only disappoint you and hurt everyone you love." It was the only time I'd seen her cry, and I don't even think she knew she was doing it. Tears flowed freely down her cheeks as she yelled at me and destroyed my work. "Do yourself a favor, Brittany. Forget this foolishness and focus on the things that matter."

I'd cried and pleaded for her to stop, but she was like a

woman possessed as she shredded my artwork into pieces before gathering up the wooden box and brushes. "Those are mine," I cried. "He gave them to me."

That stopped her. With my precious things in her hands, she stared at me and shook her head slowly. "You're just like him." And then to herself, she added, "Lord help me." And left the room.

I never saw my paintbrushes after that. And I never again painted. *Although…*

I dismissed the thought before it could take root as an actual idea because the truth was, ever since my mother died, it was as if a part of me opened up again. The part that itched to hold a paintbrush in my fingers once more.

But the idea was silly. I was just tired. It was only ten o'clock on a Saturday night, but considering work functions were pretty much the gist of my social outings, it was way past time for me to get into bed.

My phone vibrated with an incoming video call before I could push myself up from the floor. Jessie.

I hit the button to accept the call and her face filled the screen. "Hey. Didn't I just see you?"

"That was hours ago." She waved a hand and laughed. "I've already been home and—"

"I don't need to know." I cut her off before she could tell me about the amazing sex she'd no doubt had when they'd left the club. To be fair, I did kind of want to know, because hearing about my friends' amazing sex lives was as close as I seemed to get to any action of my own these days. Still. I was pretty sure I could fill in the blanks on my own.

"Okay," Jessie conceded. "But you do know that it could be you having amazing sex, Britt."

I couldn't help it; I laughed out loud. "And how is that?" I pushed up from the floor and made my way to the kitchen to feed Sheldon. "It's not as if I have a lot of opportunities." I poured food into the cat's bowl. "I don't see a man around here, do you?" I panned the camera around my very empty home. "No man."

"What about Trent?"

I almost tripped over the air when Jessie said his name. "Pardon?"

"Trent," she said again, as if I hadn't heard her. "Trent Thomas."

"I know who Trent is."

"I thought maybe you did." She wiggled her eyebrows.

"What the hell is that supposed to mean?"

I flipped off the lights behind me as I made my way to my bedroom.

"Oh, come on, Britt. I saw the way you looked at him."

"I didn't—"

"And the way he looked at you."

That stopped me. *Had he been looking at me?* I couldn't even pretend. I knew he had.

"He was there with a…" My tongue tripped over the word *woman*. Trista was barely legal. "Date," I finished, settling on a word.

"You know as well as I do that doesn't mean anything. He's into you, Britt. Anyone can see it." Jessie grinned.

Despite knowing better, I allowed myself for just a second to entertain the idea that she might be right.

But only a second, because Trent Thomas and I were never going to happen.

"He's not my type." I pulled back the comforter on my perfectly made bed and slid between the sheets.

"He's one hundred percent your type, and you know it."

She wasn't wrong. Trent was exactly the type of man I would be interested in. Primarily because he also wasn't looking for anything more than an *arrangement*. That's what I typically called my *relationships* with men. Both parties knew there was nothing and would never be anything serious. Sex and the occasional dinner date. Accompaniment to work functions at times. But mostly, sex. It had always worked for me in the past, although admittedly it had been quite some time since my last *arrangement*.

"Good night, Jessie." I exaggerated a yawn.

"Admit that I might be right," she said. "Admit that you're into him."

"Will you let me go to bed if I do?"

She nodded.

"Fine." I laughed. "I admit he's handsome, and you might be right."

She let out a whoop, and I knew it wouldn't be the last I was going to hear about this particular subject. Especially considering we were scheduled to have girls' lunch the next day.

"Goodnight, Jessie. I'll see you tomorrow."

The minute I disconnected the call, I knew sleep would be elusive. I'd managed to forget about Trent Thomas and that sinful smile while I took a trip down memory lane with my father's paintings, but one simple reminder and the only thing filling my mind when I closed my eyes was the way he looked at me and the heat that had filled every single lonely corner of me when our hands connected.

Shit.

There was no help for it.

I rolled over and fished out my most consistent sexual companion from my nightstand. It didn't take long before the familiar vibration between my legs was the only thing I could focus on as an orgasm built deep inside me. I came hard a few moments later, Trent's name on my lips.

Chapter Three

I'D SLEPT LIKE SHIT.

After dropping Trista off and returning to the hotel penthouse I was temporarily calling home, I'd taken matters into my own hands in a long, hot shower where every single image of the woman I wanted to have pressed up against the slick tiles was Brittany. Visions of her creamy white skin, water streaming down her back, between her tight ass cheeks, drove me. I came hard in a violent shudder.

I stayed under the hot water long after in an effort to clear my head of the woman who'd completely consumed my thoughts. It was ridiculous. I hardly knew a thing about her.

She was friends with Jessie.

Held in the highest regard by one of my best friends and smartest businessmen I knew, which meant she herself was extremely intelligent.

She was composed. Reserved and controlled, unlike most women I knew.

Gorgeous. No. Stunning. Brittany was beautiful in a way that made it hard to look away from her.

And those eyes. They were the most piercing shade of light

blue, but they darkened at times, too. Would they get even darker when she was turned on? I craved the knowledge.

These were the thoughts and questions that consumed me hour after hour as I tossed and turned, unable to think of much of anything else. Maybe I should have taken Trista up on her offer to go up to her apartment. Even after rejecting her in the car, which I'd tried to do as nicely as possible considering her mouth was wrapped around my cock, she was still willing to fuck me.

Certainly, if I'd taken her up on that offer, I would be properly relaxed and probably able to succumb to sleep. But I hadn't even considered it. Trista wasn't Brittany.

Not even close. And maybe I'd never have Brittany in my bed, but until I got her out of my head…well, my hand would have to do.

It was a poor substitute, and when I finally pulled myself from my bed after only a few hours of restless sleep, the only thing I was thinking about was coffee. And lots of it.

Normally on a Sunday, I'd fire up my laptop and get some work done. If I was concerned about *balance* in my life, I might have a golf game lined up with potential business partners, or in the winter, a day of skiing. But lately, I'd tried a different approach when it came to finding a work-life balance. And after I drank the majority of the pot of thick coffee I'd brewed and poured a cup to go, it was finally time.

Volunteering at the seniors' home, The Pines, was probably the last place any of my friends or colleagues would expect to find me—which was also why I hadn't told anyone—but I liked it more than even I'd expected to. When I walked through the sliding glass doors, I felt at home in a way that I hadn't felt since I was a teenager living with my own grandparents. When they passed away over five years ago—within a few months of each other, as if one couldn't live without the other—it felt like a piece was missing in my life.

Not anymore.

I'd only been volunteering for a few weeks, but the seniors at the Pines had already started to feel like friends. And in some cases, family.

"Good morning, Rose." The tiny woman with the fluffy white head of hair was the first to welcome me when I stepped through the door. "You're looking beautiful today. Did you just have your hair done?" I bent down to kiss her cheek as she giggled.

"You're such a charmer, Trent. Just like my George used to be."

"It's easy to be so charming with a beautiful lady like you."

She giggled again, and I winked as I made my way through the room. I greeted everyone in turn, even the crankier residents whom I still hadn't won over. But it was Florence and Roy Sisson who I sat down with.

"Here you go, Roy." I handed him the paper cup of coffee I'd brought with me. "Nice and strong, just the way you like it."

"You can't drink that." Florence smacked his hand lightly but her eyes twinkled. "You'll be bouncing off the walls."

"She likes to keep me quiet and demure." Roy winked dramatically and took a drink of the coffee. "You can't keep me down, woman." He laughed and kissed his wife's hand.

I enjoyed all of the seniors, but Flo and Roy were different. They reminded me of my own grandparents in the cute way they teased each other, took care of each other and seemed to be still completely devoted to each other. I had never been interested in a relationship myself, but if I ever changed my mind, I would want the type of love that Flo and Roy shared. They just felt good to be around. Like home.

"What did you get up to last night, Trent?" Florence had given up trying to convince Roy not to drink the coffee and was focused on me. "Certainly a handsome young man like yourself had a date or—"

"They don't call it dating," Roy interrupted. "It's *hooking up*."

I tried not to laugh.

"Tell me," he said to me. "Does she have a tight little— "

"Roy!"

"What?" The older man shrugged and took his wife's hand. "I'm old, Flo. Not dead. Besides, you know I only have eyes for you." He pressed a kiss to her hand and wiggled his bushy eyebrows. "It's only ever been you."

They really were super cute.

"No date," I lied. Sort of. "And it wasn't anything very exciting. Just a work function."

"Trent." Flo's voice turned serious. "Why aren't you married?"

"Wow." I laughed. "I wasn't expecting that this morning."

"Flo," Roy chastised. "Maybe he's gay. There's a lot of that these days, you know. Men can like men and—"

"Yes." She cut him off with a shake of her head. "I know how it works. But our Trent here is not gay. Are you?"

"Nope." I chuckled. "Not gay."

"I knew it." Flo brightened. "Which is why I'm going to introduce you to Sally's granddaughter. She's a—"

"Whoa." I held up my hand and moved to get up from the chair. The very last thing I needed was a setup.

"I know what you're going to say." Flo stopped me with a small but surprisingly strong hand on the arm. "But Sally's granddaughter is a nice girl. She has a good job and—"

"A tight little—"

"Roy!"

The older man shrugged and looked properly chastised. But when Florence wasn't looking, he opened his eyes wide and nodded in my direction.

"Flo," I tried to pull my arm away, "I really do appreciate your concern about my love life, but—"

"Of course, dear."

She looked at me with so much care and concern in her eyes that it stopped me. When was the last time anyone had looked at me like that? Not since my own grandparents.

"Trent, I know we haven't known you long," she said. "But Roy and I have come to think of you as our own grandson."

Next to her, Roy nodded, and it was almost my undoing. I was moments away from agreeing to the blind date and only bad things would come from that. Of that much, I was certain.

"It's only because we care that we want to see you settled down with—"

"I have a girlfriend."

The words flew out of my mouth before I could stop them. I immediately wanted to take them back, but Florence was beaming and Roy was looking at me with appreciation and maybe just the smallest bit of suspicion.

Flo clapped her hands. "This is perfect," she said. "I can't wait to meet her. You'll bring her by so we can meet her, won't you?"

"Of course he will," Roy answered for me.

I nodded, but I had no idea where I was going to produce a girlfriend for them. Of course, I could just wait and tell them we'd broken up—

"And if it doesn't work out," Roy interrupted my thoughts, "there's always Sally's granddaughter."

It wasn't very often that I was the first person to arrive for our girlfriend meetings. More often than not, I was caught up with work and running late, even on the weekends. To be fair, it was more likely on the weekends because my assistant wasn't around to hold me to my appointments.

But I hadn't felt the same pull to work all the crazy hours

lately. More and more, I found myself leaving the office long before my usual seven or eight, and an entire Sunday morning had gone by and I had only answered one email from my work account.

Which was why I found myself at the restaurant a full fifteen minutes before our lunch date. It turned out that without work filling my weekends, I didn't really have much to do and there was only so much cuddling Sheldon would tolerate. About ten minutes, to be specific.

I'd spent the hour before lunch wandering in and out of the shops in the downtown of Aspen Valley. It had been years since I'd set foot in almost any of the little stores, and they'd changed quite a bit. Aspen Valley was just far enough from the city in the mountains, with a world-class ski hill for the winter months and plenty of upscale golf courses for the summer season, that it was one of the hottest resort town destinations in North America. Because of its proximity to the city and an international airport, Aspen Valley had more recently become home to a number of prestigious companies whose executives and owners preferred to live where they could also play instead of a big, faceless city.

Of course, there were the *locals*, otherwise known as the people who were born and raised in Aspen Valley. People like my girlfriends and me. When the wealthy *city people* started moving to town, there was some initial animosity but most of those negative feelings had passed as the growth of the town had benefited everyone in a positive way. My own group of best friends was an excellent example of that.

I sipped at my ice water and signaled the waitress when, a moment later, I saw Sandy and Abby walking down the street. I ordered a coffee with Irish cream for Sandy and a martini for Abby. As a group, we were very predictable and always drank the same thing.

"What is…" Abby stopped when she saw me and dropped

her mouth in mock shock as she stood frozen in the center of the restaurant. "Is it a special occasion?"

I tipped my head and rolled my eyes before jumping up and opening my arms for a hug. "Nice to see you, too."

Abby hugged me hard. "You know it's amazing to see you. Always."

I moved from her arms to Sandy's. She was almost half a foot shorter than me and petite, but she probably gave the best hugs out of all of us. As the mother of two young girls and a widow of almost five years, Sandy joked that she did more than her fair share of hugging in order to get so good at it. Either way, I was happy to be on the receiving end of her warmth.

"Seriously," Abby said as we took our seats. "You're never here first. Are you feeling okay?"

She was joking, but there was a thread of concern in her voice as well that I couldn't miss.

"Honestly, I'm fine. I'm just starting to think that I might like to do something more with my time than work."

"Like a certain very sexy man?"

I whipped around to see Jessie had arrived. There was a sparkle in her eye as she wiggled her eyebrows.

"Sorry," she said to me. "I couldn't resist."

"Who's the sexy man?" Darla followed shortly behind Jessie, gave me a kiss on the cheek as she made her way around the table, and sat across from me.

The woman had radar when it came to any discussion of men. Ever since we were young and all became close, the boys had been drawn to Darla. Maybe it was her free spirit or her easy way of just being herself, but to this day, men were attracted to her like bees to nectar.

But despite having her choice of men, Darla continued to choose none of them. At least not longer than a month or so. The moment a man made any designs on getting serious, she moved on. We were the only two in our group to never marry.

"Are you having sexy times with a sexy man?" Darla asked, earning me a raised eyebrow from the waitress as she dropped off the two drinks and took the two new orders for Darla and Jessie. A whiskey and a glass of white wine. Same as always.

I once more contemplated adding a shot of vodka to my soda water. It was a thought I was entertaining more and more often lately. It must be all the talk about men. Or more specifically, one man.

"I am *not* having sexy times with a man." I shot Jessie a look. The last thing I needed was her telling them all about—

"But she should." Jessie interrupted my thoughts, as if she'd read them. "He's *so* sexy and he's totally into her."

I probably should have put a stop to it, but I didn't have the energy to interrupt while Jessie recounted her version of the events of the night before, including how he looked at me, the way he spoke to me, and the apparent reaction I had to him. I had to admit, her version of the events was far more exciting than my own.

Or the truth.

Was it the truth?

"So?" Abby looked at me. "Is this your—"

"We should order." I caught the attention of the waitress, who immediately presented herself at the table. "I'm starving." I steered the conversation away from the inevitable question that was no doubt on the very tip of Abby's tongue. After all, it had been her idea a few months ago to make a *go for it* pact, which was basically her way of us giving each other permission to act as if we were in our twenties again and have the same kind of fun we had years ago before our lives got…serious.

Truthfully, the pact—as silly as I thought it was—had given her the permission to spend a weekend with Phillip Conrad, the crazy-hot billionaire who was her *one who got away*, and now they were happily shacked up and having amazing sex every night. The pact had also given Jessie the courage to accept a late-night ride home from her diner from a mysterious man on a motorcycle that had resulted in some roadside sexy times that had turned into the very best thing that had ever happened to her—her college-aged twins the only exception. That mysterious man also happened to be my boss, which was the only reason I thought it was okay for my friend to get on the back of his bike in the middle of the night.

Not that she knew that at the time.

Based on the *success* of the pact for two of my best friends, I wasn't surprised in the least that it had come up for me, especially after Jessie's interrogation about Trent. Still, I didn't love the idea of *going for it*. I liked to be in control. *I* called the shots. It's how I'd always done things. And sure, it was part of the reason I was single. I liked it that way. I was fully in control if I was the only one I had to worry about.

Still…the idea of having some of the same crazy, hot sex that Abby and Jessie told us about on our weekly girls' dates *was* appealing. It had been a very long time since I'd had any actual male company—and my vibrator definitely didn't count.

And Trent *was* sinfully sexy.

Never mind the way he looked at me as though he could eat me up.

I wouldn't say no.

Dammit.

And that's exactly why I needed to make this decision on my own. I would not be pressured into it. If I was going to do this, it would be on my terms. Completely.

"I've decided that I'm going to *go for it* with Trent," I announced to the table as the waitress finished taking Sandy's order. I swallowed and added, "I'll have the Cobb salad."

Chapter Four

MONDAY MORNINGS at the office were usually my favorite time of the week. The start of a new week. The promise of so much unfulfilled potential. Mostly, my coworkers and pretty much all my friends thought I was crazy. But I *loved* Mondays.

Probably because I had zero social life on the weekends.

The thought hit me for the very first time as I pushed my way through the glass doors of the MultiTech offices, unusually late for the start of the day. For the first time in recent memory, I wasn't looking forward to going in to work. Not that there was anything else I'd rather be doing. There wasn't. But that was only because I didn't have any actual hobbies.

But maybe that could change. I still hadn't done anything with my father's paintings. They still sat on my living room floor, where I passed them a dozen times a day. And every single time I passed them, I had the same thought: *Why not?*

Why not pick up a paintbrush again and give it a try? I used to love painting. It had made me feel...free and *light*. The day my mom freaked out and took away my supplies was the last time I'd ever picked up a brush. Looking back, it was also the last day I'd felt that way.

Maybe it was time to try it again.

But first, I had bigger problems. Like the fact that I'd told my girlfriends that I'd already made the decision to *go for it* with Trent Thomas.

Why had I said that?

I barely knew the man. I'd hardly even spoken to him, and now I was supposed to be having all kinds of hot and crazy sex with him because Abby and Jessie got it in their head that acting like we were twenty again was the only way to feel young.

Not that I hated the idea of hot sex with Trent.

Not even a little.

But it's not like I could just walk up to him and say, "Hey, Trent. My friends have this crazy idea that if we just toss our inhibitions and common sense aside the way we did when we were young, that we'll have the best time of our lives. So I'm going to need to take you home so we can start working our way through the Kama Sutra."

Yeah. No. That wasn't happening.

Besides, all of this was based on the assumption that Trent even wanted to have sex with *me*.

A small smile crept across my lips as I crossed the lobby toward my office. Unless I'd completely read the situation wrong, and I don't think I did, he would probably be good with the idea. After all, he was a man. I wasn't sure what it was exactly that was between us, but there was definitely something.

I was so lost in my thoughts—and okay, my fantasies of Trent naked in my bed—that I didn't notice him until I had run directly into him.

"Oh. I—" I dropped the stack of files and folders in my arm, followed by the fresh latte I'd just picked up from the coffee bar in the lobby. "Shit." The coffee landed directly on top of the papers, the milky coffee coating the work I'd taken home for the weekend—and ignored.

"Brittany! I'm so sorry." Trent dropped to his knees and, with a napkin he'd produced from somewhere, started to mop up the mess. "I didn't see you. I'm sorry. I was just…"

"It's okay." I knelt next to him and tried to fish out the papers that hadn't been completely ruined. It didn't take me long to realize the futility of the task. I sat back on my heels and shook my head while Trent worked at blotting the papers, smearing the print, tearing the papers, and just generally making a bigger mess of what would be able to be reprinted without too much trouble.

I couldn't help myself, but watching him work so feverishly, especially because it was as much my fault as it was his, struck me as hilarious. A laugh bubbled up from my throat. I immediately clapped my hand over my mouth, but it was too late.

Trent stopped what he was doing and looked up slowly. He cocked an eyebrow in question.

"Sorry." Maybe it was nerves. Not that I ever felt nervous, but Trent…well, something was different about this guy. Either way, I tried to swallow my laughter, but I couldn't help it. Seeing him in his dress pants and tailored shirt, on his knees, wiping milky coffee all over the place and making an even bigger mess, was just too funny. I shook my head, but the laughter wouldn't stop.

Trent watched on, amused, the soaked napkin in his hand as he waited for my laughter to die down. "I have to assume there was nothing important that I destroyed this morning."

I shook my head as I worked hard to pull myself together. "Nothing that can't be reprinted."

"So you were letting me stress out for nothing?" His eyebrows knitted together in an attempt to look stern, but I simply burst out laughing again.

Trent shook his head with a chuckle. "I had no idea I had this kind of effect on you."

Oh, he had an effect on me, that was for sure.

"I have to be honest. This wasn't the type of effect I was hoping for."

The laughter died on my lips. *What?*

"Don't stop," he said. "I like watching you laugh. It's…"

The moment was gone, but a new one presented itself. Maybe it was the whole *go for it* thing or the fact that we were kneeling across from each other in the middle of the lobby, or… well, it didn't matter what the reason was—I needed to know. "It's what?"

He looked me straight in the eyes, and there it was again. That crazy stomach-turning, soul-searching stare that looked right past all of my walls and to the heart of me.

He licked his bottom lip as it quirked up into a sly grin. "It's really fucking sexy."

It was the first word that came to mind when it came to Brittany. Hell, it was the *only* word. It was the only way to describe her.

She'd looked smoking hot at the party the other night with her tight black dress and so much creamy skin showing. But nothing could have prepared me for how sexy Brittany was when she laughed. The sound did intense things to my body. It was a good thing I wasn't standing because I wasn't sure I'd be able to control the instant physical reaction she had on me.

Damn.

I would have kept her laughing all day, if I had my way. Except now she stared at me with a strange look I couldn't quite read. *Had I crossed a line?*

"Well, I don't know how sexy I could possibly be on the

floor of the lobby with coffee all over my blouse, but hey." She shrugged.

My gaze moved to her blouse, and I noticed for the first time that it, too, was stained with coffee. *Shit.* Although I was not complaining about the way the sheer fabric skimmed over her pert breasts, the faintest outline of a lacy bra underneath.

"I'm so sorry, Brittany." I gathered up her ruined papers and got to my feet before offering her a hand. As soon as her skin touched mine, I didn't want to let go.

"It's not your—"

"I really owe you—"

We spoke at the same time.

"You owe me?" She tilted her head, her hand still in mine.

"Of course I do." I tightened my hold on her, just the tiniest bit. "After all, I crashed into you, ruined your work, and your blouse. Maybe I could—"

"Do me a favor?"

A favor? This was turning out to be a very interesting Monday morning after all. "What kind of favor?"

Brittany looked down at our hands as if she'd noticed them together for the first time. She pulled away. "It's kind of silly really, but…" She glanced around.

We'd attracted more than one gawker who was looking for some kind of juicy gossip to take back to the lunchroom. And if I'd been able to keep touching her, there was no doubt we'd give the onlookers more than a few things to gossip about.

"Can we talk about it in my office?"

There was nothing I'd like more than to have her alone in her office. Up against the wall, my mouth on hers, my hands divesting her of her ruined blouse, my mouth on her tits… "Of course."

A few moments later, she was closing the door behind us in her office, the ruined papers had been dumped in the garbage bin, and with a quick pull of a cord, the blinds to her large picture window that faced out into the main office area were closed.

When she was ready, Brittany turned around, her arms behind her on the desk, so she was leaning back in a power pose that made it clear that she was the boss. Or at least that she *thought* she was. It was an important distinction.

I took a step toward her and crossed my arms loosely over my chest. "So, what is it I can help you with?"

No less than fifty things that involved the two of us naked on her oversized mahogany desk, preferably with her *bent over* her desk, raced through my brain. Oh yes, there were definitely a few things I could help her with.

"Before I tell you, I want you to know that it doesn't mean anything, okay? I just don't want you to read anything more into it than there is."

Interesting.

I took another step toward her, drawn to her as if there were a string pulling me close. My eyes locked on hers so I didn't miss the way they blazed darker. I noticed everything when it came to this woman.

"My friends and I have this…" She waved a hand in the air. "Well, it's hard to explain. But it's this whole thing and it's just about having fun and not being so serious and…well…"

I liked seeing her flustered because I had the distinct impression it didn't happen very often. "You want me to help you have fun?" My lips twitched up in a grin. I could definitely help with a little fun.

"Yes. I mean, no. I mean…look. As I said, it doesn't have to be anything. But I just wanted to let you know that I may have told them a little bit of a white lie."

Even more interesting.

"What did you tell them?"

She shrugged. "It's not a big deal, okay. I just kind of implied that we were having sex."

Whoa.

Whatever it was that I was expecting, it was not that.

"A lot of it," she continued. "And really hot sex, up against the wall kind of stuff."

And I was definitely not expecting *that.*

I stood completely still for a moment, letting the information process. It took longer than I expected. Finally, I blinked. "So what is it you need from me if you've already told them this information?"

She took a breath and shook her head a little with a shrug. "I just thought that since you said you owed me that…"

"I could play along?"

She exhaled. "Or…"

"Interesting." That didn't even begin to describe the situation. Still, it was a place to start. "The way I see it," I continued, "we could approach this one of two ways. Because you're right, I do owe you a favor."

She nodded, visibly relieved.

"The first—I could go along with whatever it is you told your friends. We're having sex? Sure. I'll play along. But that makes you a liar, and you don't strike me as the lying type."

I took a step closer until we were close enough that I could smell her perfume. It was unexpectedly soft and floral. Her breath came quickly, as if my proximity knocked her off guard. I liked it. I liked that I left this perfectly in control woman a little off-balance. Her breasts strained against her top with every breath. I had to force my eyes up and away from them before I got too distracted. "Or, two…" I leaned in so my lips were only inches from hers. "We could take it a step further and keep you honest."

Chapter Five

HOLY SHIT.

What had I gotten myself into? I couldn't even believe the words were coming out of my mouth when I'd asked him to... what? Have sex with me? Had *that* been what I'd asked?

No.

Of course not. I'd only asked him to play along with the story. That was all.

Was it?

With Trent standing so close, it was hard to breathe. Every time I took a breath, the scent of him filled my senses so I couldn't even think. Spicy and warm, like cinnamon and leather. He smelled powerful, and sexy as sin.

Dammit.

I was very quickly losing control of this negotiation—if you could even call it that. Still, I hated being out of control. I needed the ball back in my court. I needed to be in control of this.

"Your choice, Brittany," he said, still waiting for an answer.

It wasn't even a choice.

Of course I wanted to have sex with him. Just looking at

him had my stomach doing all kinds of funny things, and if he was even half as good as the fantasies I had with my vibrator between my legs...*oh yes*.

I reached out for his tie and pulled him even closer. "I'm not a liar."

His lips curled up in a wicked grin. "I didn't think so."

It was a damn good thing I was already leaning against the desk because when his lips met mine, I lost all feeling in my legs. They were jelly beneath me. All of the focus was on his mouth crushed against mine. Our tongues twisted together, and Trent's hand slipped up the back of my head, his fingers tangling in my hair as he tugged my head back to expose my neck.

His mouth nibbled and sucked my sensitive skin. "Damn, you taste better than I expected."

Just as quickly as his mouth was on my neck, it was gone, and both his hands were in my hair, holding my head as he pulled back and stared at me. "Just to clarify," he said, his breath coming in pants. "The favor you need is for me to have sex with you?"

"Well..."

"Sorry," he added quickly. "Super-hot, up against the wall type of sex? Is that right?"

Oh, God. Doing it would be so much better than simply talking about it.

I could only nod.

"Right," he said with a small smile. "As much as I'm on board with this, and I assure you, I am—"

I could feel his *assurance* pressing against me.

"I'm going to need to hear you say it before we take this any further. Because I'll be honest, this was the last thing I expected when I got to the office this morning."

He wasn't the only one.

With my face held between his big, strong hands, I couldn't

look away. Not that I wanted to. Now that this whole crazy thing had been initiated, the fire had been lit, and the very last thing I wanted to do was put it out. I took as deep of a breath as I could manage and exhaled slowly. "Trent," I worked hard to keep my voice level, "I want you to have sex with me."

He nodded and kissed me softly. "Sex? Or...how did you put it?" He grinned.

So cocky. So ridiculously sexy.

I reached around him, dug my fingers into his hard ass, and pulled him up against me. "Give me something to talk about."

A low growl came from deep in his throat. "Abso-fucken-loutely."

Trent scooped me up and deposited me on my desk.

Here? Now?

My brain scrambled for the pause button. I'd never had sex in my office before. How could I? An entire office of staff and employees were right outside. Never mind Shane Grant, my boss, who could walk in at any moment.

"Stop thinking about it," Trent growled, barely taking his lips off mine.

He kissed me with a hunger I'd never experienced from a lover before. As if he needed me to breathe. It was all-consuming and made it hard to think. I couldn't formulate my thoughts. All I could think about was him. Me. Now.

"But...we're—"

"I told you to stop thinking." He made his point with a slight bite on my bottom lip. Immediately, he sucked it between his own lips to soften the pain, and a shot of desire slammed through me. "Brittany?"

He waited for me to look up at him. He held my chin between his thumb and forefinger before rubbing his thumb against the spot on my lip he'd just bit. Pulses of desire mixed with the slightest trace of pain worked their way through every cell of my body.

"I know you're used to being in charge," he said when I looked at him. "But if this is going to work, you're going to have to listen to me."

Listen to him? That wasn't part of the deal. Of course, there had been no actual *deal.* This whole thing had all started on a whim. Maybe I should have thought it through? Maybe I...

Stop.

What *was* the harm in letting him take control and call a few shots? I'd never actually experienced that before, and... well, maybe the girls *were* right? What was the real harm in letting go a little? There wasn't. Besides, we'd already determined I wasn't going to be a liar, so...*just go for it.*

"Do we have a deal?"

Why the hell not? "Yes."

That was all I needed to hear.

Forcing Brittany to relinquish control, even a little bit, was quite possibly the biggest turn-on I'd ever experienced in my whole life. Fuck. This woman was the very epitome of control. Which was exactly why this was going to be amazing.

She was the complete opposite of almost every other woman I'd been with in the last few years. The difference was, Brittany was a *woman.* Not a girl. She knew exactly what she wanted and how to get it.

Like, ask me for a favor.

And what a favor it was. What hot-blooded man in his right mind would be able to turn that down? None. Certainly not one with any friggin' sense.

With Brittany seated on her shiny, perfectly clean desk, her long, straight, blonde hair hung over her shoulders, I couldn't help but think what she'd look like with her tits out, her hair draped over her nipples, like beautiful shiny curtains.

Damn.

There'd be time for that. But right now, we needed to cement this deal before she changed her mind. And the best way I could think to do that was to give her an earth-shattering orgasm.

I saw the way her eyes darted to the door where her assistant could walk in any minute. It would need to be quick. As much as I wanted her to let go and put all of her trust in me that we weren't going to get caught, I knew it was going to take time. A woman like Brittany didn't blindly give up control. Not even close.

With my fingers still holding her chin in place, I turned her head so she could no longer see the door. Then I spun her completely on the shiny wood surface so she wouldn't be tempted to look away. I knew it would drive her crazy. But I planned to do that for myself shortly.

I kissed her hard, forcing myself to hold back. She tasted sweeter than I could ever have imagined. The taste of her was intoxicating and like a drug, I needed more. Still, I held off. I was a demanding lover by nature. I expected a lot from my partner and gave as much as I got. Probably more. But this needed to be about her. Completely about her.

I threaded one hand through her hair and tugged back on her head, just a little, as I devoured her mouth, possessing her with my tongue. My other hand moved to the zipper of her dress pants, sliding it down. When she was completely breathless from my kiss, I slid both hands over her hips and into her pants. "Lift," I ordered.

Brittany did as I asked, and a moment later, I'd shed her of her pants.

"Damn." I looked up from the black lace panties she wore. "You knew exactly what you were doing today, didn't you?"

Confusion lined her face for a moment before she followed

my gaze back to her lace-encased pussy. Brittany laughed. "You think I wore those for you?"

"You didn't?"

"I don't wear anything for a man." Her pale-blue eyes flashed with defiance.

We'd see about that.

But I believed her. The lingerie was for her. My pleasure was an added benefit. For me. But Brittany was the type of woman who wouldn't do anything she didn't want to. Which was why it was going to be particularly rewarding when she did something just for me. And I was confident that would happen. Soon.

I turned my attention to the task at hand, and with one hand on each of her creamy white thighs, spread them wide.

"Trent, I—"

I pressed one finger against her lips while another traced the elastic of those pretty black panties. She shuddered under my attentions and closed her eyes, but there were no further protests.

I kept my finger against her lips as I rubbed my thumb over the lace, against her clit.

She cried out and her eyes flew open in shock.

"If you don't want anyone to know," I grinned, "you might want to try to be a bit quieter." I kissed her again to help her with the effort to stay quiet. This time, while my tongue explored her mouth and my hand held her head still, my free hand pushed past the boundary of her panties to the soft, bare flesh of her pussy. I murmured my appreciation against her mouth but didn't take my mouth from hers as I slipped a finger inside her wet, hot heat.

Brittany gasped into my mouth. Her body tensed for a quick moment and then relaxed against my touch. My thumb delivered a consistent pressure to her clit while my finger worked in and out of her pussy. Slowly at first, and then, when she started to groan, faster. I hooked my finger up inside her to hit her most sensitive spot.

She cried out, but I swallowed it with my kiss, tempted not to. It would be extra hot if everyone in the lobby heard her pleasure as she came. But I didn't want to push her too hard. Not yet.

Still, I didn't relent my attentions to her pussy as I felt her body tighten around my finger.

Brittany pulled her mouth from mine to mutter, "I'm going to come, Trent. Oh my God. I'm going to come."

"That's the idea, baby. Come hard for me."

She did as she was told, unable to do anything but, as I increased the pressure on her clit. She buried her head in my neck to muffle her cry as she came apart around me.

Fuck. Watching her lose control was the sexiest thing I'd ever witnessed. My cock throbbed hard for a release of its own, but it wasn't the time.

When she'd just about come back to her senses, I wriggled my finger, still inside her, and flicked the hard bud of her clit with my thumb one last time. She gasped and her eyes widened.

I could only grin in response before slowly withdrawing my finger from her now completely soaked pussy.

"Trent. That was…it was…"

I sucked my finger dry of her juices, before finishing her statement for her. "The hottest thing I've seen in a very long time."

Shit, she tasted good. Immediately, I wanted more. A lot more.

Before Brittany could respond, the phone on her desk buzzed. "Ms. Donahue?" Her assistant's voice filled the office.

Her breath still came in pants, but Brittany reached around her and pressed the button on her phone. "Yes, Julie?"

"Your nine o'clock meeting is here. I was just wondering if—"

"I'll be out in a few minutes," Brittany interrupted.

I couldn't help but smile as I watched her, still mostly naked from the waist down, go into work mode. Sexy didn't even begin to describe this woman.

"I'm just finishing up with Mr. Thomas."

I cocked an eyebrow as she turned her attention back to me. "Oh, we're nowhere near finished."

Brittany hopped off her desk and reached for her pants, but I already had them in my hand. She tilted her head. "Trent, I have a meeting. I—"

I silenced her with a kiss. Damn, I liked shutting her up that way. Especially because she responded so readily to my kisses.

I backed her up against her desk again and reached between her legs. The lace of her panties was soaked through.

"I'll take those." I stepped back. "For these." I held her dress pants up.

"You want my panties?"

"Most definitely."

She looked as if she were going to object, but her lips twitched up in a smile and she quickly removed them and handed them to me.

I tucked them into my pocket and kissed her one more time. Mostly because now that I had a taste, I truly couldn't get enough. "I'll see you tonight." I turned for the door.

"Tonight? But I—"

I looked over my shoulder and held her eyes. "You said you'd listen to me, Brittany."

"But...I..."

"Seven," I said. "Hourglass."

Chapter Six

SOMEHOW I MADE it through my day. But I wasn't sure how I did it when every single time I sat—or stood…or walked…or, did anything—my bare pussy rubbed against my slacks and set every nerve ending alight. Again.

Damn. I hadn't come that way in a very long time.

Maybe it was the fact that it was completely taboo to have sex in my office. Or the fact that it had been a few months since I'd had a man's touch on me instead of just my vibrator. But I didn't think so. It was Trent.

Yes. It was definitely Trent.

I still couldn't believe I'd just asked him point-blank to have sex with me.

No.

I'd asked him to play along with my little white lie. But it had been *his* idea to make an honest woman out of me. Judging by our quick little rendezvous, it had been a damn good idea, too.

I couldn't wait to see what came next. Because as good as that had been, it had only been a taste and I needed more.

I almost laughed aloud at myself, because I'd never once in

my life felt that way about a man, let alone one who was simply doing me a favor.

And what a favor it was.

By five o'clock, I'd given up. Focusing on work was completely pointless and I still had a few hours to kill before meeting Trent at Hourglass, a trendy cocktail bar downtown. He'd said seven.

He'd said.

Because I'd agreed to listen to him. A thrill ran up my spine at the thought. When had I *ever* listened to a man? Never. Even in my short-lived, sex-only relationships, I'd been the one in charge. And it's not that what Trent and I were doing was anything like that. But still. I couldn't deny it was an incredible turn-on to have someone else call the shots.

And most importantly, I wasn't going to be lying to my friends when I reported back to them about how things had gone with Trent. Despite the fact that I'd been quick to tell them that little untruth, I wasn't a liar. Especially not when it came to my best friends. Those girls had been through it all with me. And I with them. They were my family, and I would never do anything that would hurt them. Never.

Feeling a little guilty, I hit the button to bring up the group chat.

Anyone up for a chat?

Seconds later, Sandy's face filled my screen. I laughed as I accepted the call.

"Tell me something to make my boring day more exciting." She groaned. "Seriously, I love these kids, but I really need to get out more." She sighed. "Maybe a vacation. Alone. Oh, what bliss. Can you even imagine? Oh my goodness, of course you can," she added quickly. "Look who I'm talking to. You lucky thing. You always get to be alone."

I grinned wickedly. "Except I wasn't alone in my office this morning."

It took Sandy a second to catch on to what I was saying. But when she did, she shrieked. Right as Abby joined the call.

"What's going on? Why is Sandy screaming?"

I laughed. "I was just telling her that I might not have been completely alone in my office this morning."

"What does that mean?"

"Yes," Sandy added. "I mean, I think I know what it means. But what does it mean? Is it...oh!" Her hand flew to her mouth. "It *is*."

"It is what?" Abby asked right as Jessie joined the call.

"What are we talking about?" she asked.

Sandy was quick to answer. "Just about whether Brittany was alone in her office this morning or not."

"Which she clearly was not," Abby joined in.

"Trent?" Jessie got straight to the point. "In your *office*?"

The fact that all my friends knew exactly how big a deal having any kind of hook-up in my office was impressed me. They knew my office was a sacred space. I didn't screw around with my livelihood.

Until now.

"Seriously?" Jessie asked. "I mean, I kind of thought...well, I wasn't sure what I thought. But I guess I didn't think you would work so quickly."

"I told you I was going to go for it, and I did." I tried for nonchalant, but I wasn't sure how successful I was with it. "And, it...well, let's just say if this morning was any indication of what will go on, you ladies were definitely on to something." Every word I spoke was true. One hundred percent. This may have started with the tiniest of lies, but there was nothing but the truth in what I'd just told them.

"Details!" Sandy's face got uncomfortably close to the screen.

"Details about what?" Darla joined the chat. "What are we talking about?"

"Oh, just about Brittany here having some crazy-ass sex in her *office* with Trent." Jessie was quick to fill her in.

"It wasn't sex." I hated to disappoint them, but one little tiny lie was enough. Nothing but the truth now. "But it was… well, it was close. And…" I blushed. Hard.

"You came." It wasn't a question, and Abby looked more than a little pleased with herself.

I nodded. "Very hard."

"Fuck ya!"

"Good for you."

"Ohhh…I don't know if I remember what that feels like." Sandy realized her comment and quickly shook her head with a backtrack. "I mean," she said. "Yay, you."

"Your turn is coming, Sandy." Darla's features turned serious. "I promise you. If I have to make it my personal mission to make sure you have an orgasm in this decade, I will do it myself."

Everyone burst out laughing.

"I don't think it will come to that," Jessie said after a moment.

"You don't know that." Darla was still very serious, and I was certain she meant every word she'd said.

"Thank you?" Sandy said cautiously. "But we're talking about Brittany and her latest orgasm."

All the virtual-teleconferencing eyes shifted back to me. "Latest?" Jessie asked. "I want details. About all of them."

I really hoped there would be more to give her, and soon. But as it was, I filled the girls in on all the juicy details of my early morning office experience.

Okay, not *all* the details. I left the part about agreeing to listen to Trent out. After all, they wouldn't have believed me if I'd told them. I didn't *listen* to anyone. And I couldn't help but feel as if I was already walking on a thin rope when it came to believability. Even though every single thing that had happened in my office had been very, very real.

I signed off the conversation thirty minutes later with the promises of more details, should there be any.

And I would move heaven and earth to make sure there were more.

I had just enough time to run home and change my clothes before my meeting with Trent. Seven p.m. at the Hourglass. Something told me I didn't want to be late.

She was late.

I should have known better.

A woman like Brittany Donahue didn't like to be told what to do.

But…no.

That was the thing.

A woman like Brittany Donahue wanted *very* much to be told what to do. That was the whole point. Power executives who'd given their whole lives to business, to success—they were used to everyone giving them exactly what they wanted, when they wanted, and *how* they wanted.

But that's not how I played.

And if I was going to play—and it looked like I was—she would have to play by my rules.

I called the shots. She'd do as I said. At least when it came to the bedroom. Or in this case—up against the wall.

Hadn't she made that particular point very clear? Hot sex up against the wall.

I'd be more than happy to deliver.

And bent over her desk. And in the back seat of my town

car. And in the hot tub of my penthouse suite. And maybe…if we got that far…in her bed.

If she showed up.

I sipped at my whiskey and tried not to look annoyed as I glanced at my phone.

Brittany was already fifteen minutes late. No text. No call.

Five more minutes and the deal was off.

Although, my cock, which had been in a semi-hard state all day after the rendezvous in her office, would disagree with me.

I sucked in a deep breath and willed my dick to settle down. I'd take care of it either way. No matter what happened. Although any backup plan wouldn't come close to sinking into the hot, sweet flesh of Brittany's pussy. That much was clear.

"Trent."

Her voice washed over me, and I looked up slowly to see Brittany in a skirt that fell just below her knees, a freshly laundered V-neck blouse tucked primly into the waistband, and a jacket hung over her arm, walking toward me.

"You're late."

"I'm sorry." She paused at the table in front of me. "I needed to go home to change."

I took my time looking her up and down, appraising every inch of her.

Fuck.

I knew I was being an asshole, but I couldn't help myself. She'd kept me waiting. Fifteen minutes was fifteen minutes too long. That was fifteen minutes I could have been enjoying her company. Fifteen minutes I could have been kissing her. Fifteen minutes I could have been *fucking* her.

"My time is valuable," I said after a moment. "Don't be late again. Not if you want me to do *you* a favor."

She bristled. And for a moment I thought I'd gone too far. After all, she didn't know it yet, but having my hands between her legs had been just as much a favor to me as it had been to her. And I wasn't even remotely done with her yet.

"I'm sorry," she said after a moment.

Something in her voice made me look up from the whiskey in my glass. Her eyes, so clear and blue, were wide and watching me. There was nothing but sincerity in her gaze.

"I really did want to change for our first…well, our first…"

"Date?" I offered.

"Is that what this is?" Her smile was small. Tentative.

I couldn't help but love it when she dropped her tough executive act for me. My cock sprang to life to see the way she nodded. I loved it when she was shy and submissive. But also, when she was a fierce, female boss. I think my body just loved every single bit of this woman. And who was I to deny that attraction?

I got to my feet and pulled out a chair for her the way I should have the moment she arrived. "Yes," I said. "Let's call this a date." I kissed her on the cheek. It was chaste, but my body certainly didn't get that message. "You look beautiful. And while I'm not thrilled about you being late, I am happy you are here." She sat, and I slid the chair in, bending to inhale the sweet scent of her hair before I retook my seat.

"Look," she said the moment I sat down. "I know this isn't exactly what you were expecting when you came to work this morning, and I wouldn't blame you if you wanted to pull out. I just had this crazy idea and…well, I don't usually make it a habit to shy away from my ideas. So I understand if this isn't what you want."

I waited for her to finish her obviously planned out and practiced little speech. I tried and failed to keep the smile off my face. "Are you done?"

She nodded and picked up her water glass for a sip.

"What makes you think that I'm the type of man who does anything I don't want to do?"

She choked and sputtered on the water. "I…"

"Just so we're clear, Brittany," I saved her. "I'm not that type of man. I *only* do things and enter into deals, or bargains or *favors*, if it's exactly what I want. Do you understand?"

She nodded but still didn't speak.

In my pants, my cock pulsed with need for her and the way she was submitting to me so freely. But I knew it wouldn't be easy. Nothing about Brittany would be easy, and that was the real attraction.

"So be sure," I continued, "I'm here because I want to be. Do you understand what that means?" I pinned her down with my gaze, so I didn't miss the challenge flare in her eyes. *Bring it.* When she didn't answer right away, I pressed. "Do you?"

"I do." She sat back as the waiter arrived and placed a vodka soda in front of her as I had pre-ordered. It was a little detail I'd picked up. Brittany didn't drink very often, but when she did, a vodka soda was her preference.

Just as I'd predicted, she picked up the cocktail and took a sip.

"I want to get one thing clear," she said smoothly as she put the glass down. "This little *favor* you're doing for me. That's all it is," she said. "A *favor*. Nothing more. There's nothing between us. Got it?"

"Completely." I sipped at my whiskey. "And just so *you* are clear, Brittany. This *favor*…" I waited until her eyes were on me, a big swallow of her cocktail in her mouth. "I meant what I said earlier. The only way it's going to work is if you listen to me. Even when your instinct tells you differently. Especially then. Understand?"

She swallowed.

Instead of answering, she drained her cocktail and set it hard on the table. Her eyes locked on mine, she nodded. "Understood."

Chapter Seven

I DID UNDERSTAND.

He wanted me to *listen to him*. But it was more than that, and we both knew it. A man like Trent Thomas needed control. It was obvious.

And it was all I could think about from the moment he'd said it earlier that morning.

Yes. I'd listen to him.

I couldn't help but acknowledge how it had felt to let go of control earlier when he had his finger inside me, his mouth on mine, making me come harder than I'd come in years. I never would have done that in any other circumstance, but some-how…when I did, it freed me.

It was no longer my decision. It wasn't my responsibility whether it was wrong or right to screw in my office. It was just…it just was.

I'd never, not one time in my entire life, given up control of…well…anything. To anyone.

But if not now, when?

And really, I'd already decided to go along with the girls' silly plan of *go with it.* So why not.

I watched his face as his lips quirked up into a grin. "I have to say," he rolled his whiskey glass between his hands, "I'm surprised."

That was a shock for me. "You are?"

He nodded. "Pleasantly so. Don't get me wrong," he added quickly. "But I really didn't think you'd agree so readily."

I took a deep breath and tilted my head just a little so my hair slipped down my back. "Honestly?"

He nodded.

"Why not?" It was the simplest statement, but it was the only way to describe what I felt. "I mean," I continued, "I'd already thrown it all out the window, asking you to do this for me, and…well, I figure I have nothing to lose."

His face contorted into a ridiculously handsome smile as he tried not to laugh. "I can't disagree with that," he said. "After all, I'd say this is a win-win for both of us. I'll be honest, Brittany. Your offer this morning took me off guard."

I wasn't blind. I knew it had.

"But it wasn't unwelcome," he continued. "And I think you know that."

Fire shot through me and directly to my core, where it burned bright and hot.

"You saw the way I looked at you," Trent said.

His eyes held me the way they always did and dammit if he wasn't right. There was a reason I'd made my proposal to him. I'd built my career on my gut instincts, and it looked like I was right again.

"I have to say, I'm glad you accepted then." I tore my gaze away from his. "But we'll need some ground rules. As I said, this isn't anything, and I don't want either of us to think for a moment it is."

He nodded.

"Sex," I continued. "That's it. No longer than a month." Long enough to satisfy the whole pact thing with my friends, but not too long. "Or sooner if either of us decides." I couldn't imagine that, but still. "No strings."

"Deal." He nodded without hesitation. "Is that it?"

I racked my brain for any other rules, but couldn't think of any. I nodded. "That's it."

"And you agree to mine?"

I sighed, already regretting it. "I already did."

"Good."

I watched as Trent drained the contents of his glass, tossed a stack of bills on the table that was at least three times what the bill should be, and stood.

He held out his hand. "Time to go."

Oh, it was time to go all right.

Literally, the only thing I'd thought about since walking out of her office that morning had been finishing what we started. I didn't really have a plan when I left the bar, only that I needed to get her alone. And quickly.

The moment she'd slid her hand in mine, so willing to trust me, again, I became a ticking time bomb. This woman drove me crazy in ways that I didn't completely understand. She was such a contrast. It was hard to keep up.

But I was up for the challenge.

With her hand still in mine, I led Brittany around the building. Fucking in an alley wasn't exactly the way I wanted the first time with Brittany to go down, but I was quickly getting to a point where I needed it to go down one way or the other.

"Where are we going?"

I took another look at the alley and turned to face her. With a tug of her hand, I pulled her close against my chest so I could kiss her. She melted into my kiss as I tugged her even closer. My cock throbbed with need in my pants, and I knew she could feel me through our thin clothes.

"You're making me crazy, woman."

Her lips twitched up in a sly grin. "Is that right?"

"You know it is." I threaded my fingers through her hair and held her head while I kissed her again. Hard. My free hand slipped down and under her skirt, where my fingers splayed over her ass.

"Fuck." The word was a growl. "Do you live close by?"

Something flashed on her face but in the dim light, I couldn't be sure.

"Not my place."

The hotel I was staying in was only a few blocks away. Too far.

I wrenched myself away from her mouth and pulled her deeper into the dark between the two buildings.

She hesitated. "Here?"

"Is that a problem?" I waited and watched as all kinds of things traveled over her face as she battled with herself. Between what she thought was *right* and what she *wanted*, I had no doubt it was quite an internal battle. "Didn't you say something about up against the wall sex?"

That was all it took. Her pupils dilated and her face transformed with need.

"I guess I did," she said with the slightest glimpse of a smile on her sexy lips.

Maybe I should have taken her deeper into the shadows between the two buildings. But the hard-on between my legs was making it hard to think—and walk. Besides, I liked the light coming from the street. I wanted to see her face when I made her come.

"Your wish is my command."

She let out a puff of air as I backed her up against the wall.

"Is that right?" She wiggled her eyebrows. "And here I

thought you wanted *me* to listen to *you*." She ran her hands down my chest, leaving a trail of flames as she got closer to my belt.

My body shuddered from her attentions, but it was a dangerous precedent to set so early on in our arrangement. There was more than one reason I wanted control in this deal. Yes, watching her come apart on my terms would be the biggest fucking turn-on I could dream of, but there was more to it. I knew better than to let a woman like Brittany call the shots when it came to something like this. Sex. That's all it was and would ever be. Which was why everything would be on my terms.

On a sharp inhale, I grabbed her hands in mine, yanked them up over her head, and pinned both wrists in one hand. "Make no mistake." I looked into her eyes. "You will be listening to me."

With her hands still in my grip, I slid the other hand down her side, taking my time to feel every sexy, perfect curve as I went. "I like the skirt," I said as my fingers danced under the short hem. "I didn't peg you for a short skirt type of woman."

"There are exceptions to every rule."

Her breath came fast. She was turned on when I took control of the situation.

"And I thought maybe this…"

Her words trailed away as I traced a finger between her legs.

Fuck. She was already wet for me.

From the moment I'd met Brittany, I'd known there was something special about her. Something that drew me to her like a moth to a friggin' flame, but I never could have expected this from her. This full-on desire and immediate, uncensored response. It was perfect. So. Fucking. Perfect.

Her panties were in the way. I needed access to her. Now. With a sharp tug, I tore the lace.

Brittany gasped.

"Better." I groaned and pressed on her clit, giving it just enough pressure to make her gasp. "I love how fucking turned on you are for me."

"You think it's for you?"

So. Much. Sass.

I kissed her until she was gasping for breath, and my fingers, still between her legs, were dripping with her juices. "Oh," I pulled away, "I *know* it's for me."

She couldn't argue with that, and I was pretty sure she didn't want to.

"I'm going to let go of your hands now." I waited until she nodded. "I want you to undo my pants." I murmured my command in her ear.

"Here?"

"Fuck yes."

I knew the element of risk, of getting caught in the office, pushed her right to the edge of her comfort zone, but this was a different kind of risk. One that made my cock painfully hard. And judging by her breath and the way she was trembling all around me, she was just as turned on.

Her breath came faster now. I pressed my finger inside her, just a little, but it was enough.

"Oh fuck."

"That's right, baby. If you liked our little appetizer this morning in your office, it's time for the main course." I released her hands. "Now."

She squeezed her eyes shut for a second, as if she needed to talk herself into what she was about to do. But when she opened them, there was no hesitation. Her long, slender fingers moved to my belt, pulling it free easily before sliding the zipper of my slacks down and releasing my throbbing dick from its confines. Her hand wrapped around my length and squeezed before starting a gentle stroke with no prompting from me.

Brittany knew exactly what she was doing because she was a woman. An incredibly sexy woman. Completely unlike the young women I usually dated who needed all of the instruction. Sure, I liked to be in charge; that wasn't a secret. But there was a very distinct difference between a girl who *needed* the direction I provided and a woman who *gave* me that power.

I couldn't remember the last time I'd ever been even remotely as turned on as I was with her.

I pulled my finger from her long enough to get a condom from my back pocket. It only took me seconds to sheath myself. "Once we do this," I said, "we're committed."

"Committed?"

I nodded. "You said no longer than a month, right?"

She narrowed her eyes. "You agreed."

"And I still do. But if we do this, I need an extension clause."

Surprise lined her face. "You want an extension clause?"

"Yes. If we both agree, we continue." I hadn't planned to put this condition on what we were doing, but without even being inside her, I knew I'd need more. *A lot* more. I couldn't risk her changing her mind before I was done with her. She was a woman of her word. I knew if she agreed, there would be no going back.

"Could I ask you why?"

"You could. But the longer we discuss it, the…" I glanced around, reminding both of us of exactly where we were and what we were about to be doing. I gripped her hips and lifted her, making her gasp. Her back was still pressed against the rough brick, but now her feet were off the ground, my cock poised and ready to enter her.

I could see the confusion on her face, but then, she shrugged a little and nodded. "Okay."

The word was hardly out of her mouth before I lowered her onto my hard cock.

She cried out as I filled her completely. I stilled inside her, waiting for her to adjust to my size.

"Holy shit, Trent." Brittany's hands gripped my shoulders. "Fuck me."

I probably should have chastised her for trying to call the shots, but I let her have that one because there was nothing I wanted and *needed* more than to do just that.

I thrust up into her. Hard.

She groaned and her legs wrapped around my waist, pulling me tighter toward her. Her heels dug into my ass, and I thrust again, harder this time. She cried out and some part of me was cognizant that we could very easily be overheard or discovered. I didn't care.

The only thing I cared about was being deep inside this woman. She took every one of my thrusts, urging me on with a squeeze, a cry. Her fingers dug into my shoulders when I increased my pace. As much as I would have liked to take my time and enjoy every second with her, there would be time for that later.

The memory of her agreement fueled me, and I fucked her harder.

"Oh, my God, Trent."

I knew it even before she said it; her body tightened around me, and Brittany moaned, "I'm going to come."

"Baby. That's the fucking idea." Relentless, I kept up my pace, until I, too, was vibrating with imminent release. "Come with me, baby. Come hard, Britt."

I kept my eyes open wide while she did just that. Her orgasm crested, hard. She cried out and as much as the sound made me crazy, I swallowed it with a kiss while I, too, took my climax.

"Fuck, Brittany," I said the moment I could form a coherent thought. "That was quite possibly the most intense orgasm I've had in a very long time." It was a massive under-statement. There was no way I'd *ever* come that hard. Ever.

Reluctantly, I set her back on the ground and smoothed her skirt down for her before tucking myself into my pants. When I was finished buckling my belt, she still hadn't spoken. When I turned to look, Brittany's head was leaning back against the wall, her eyes shut and her hands pressed flat against the brick.

Concerned, I moved in front of her and cupped her cheek. "Britt?" My thumb made small circles on her soft skin. "Are you...are you okay?"

Had I been too rough? Shit. That was the last thing I wanted. I should have kept my control and—

"I'm fine." She opened her eyes. The light blue sparkled despite the low light. "More than fine," she said. "Dammit, Trent. If I knew you could fuck like that, we would have made this deal ages ago."

Chapter Eight

MAYBE IT WAS the incredible sex Trent and I had a few days previously. Maybe it was the inspiration of seeing my father's paintings after so many years. Or maybe, I was just ready for a change. Whatever it was, I'd finally been inspired to stop at the art store and pick up some paints, a few canvases, and a sketchbook.

The canvas had been set up for over an hour already and I still wasn't sure what I wanted to paint. When I was a kid, I experimented with all kinds of things: landscapes, animals, my friends. Whatever was around and inspired me. Which was everything. But now…I didn't know where to begin.

Don't overthink it.

I always envisioned my dad's voice—or what I could remember of it—when I thought about painting advice. As if he were guiding me from…well, wherever he was. Sometimes I forgot he might be still alive, it had been so long. Mom had always talked about him as if he were dead. On the rare occasion that she actually did talk about him.

It had always been as if he didn't exist anymore. And for a

young Brittany, it had felt that way. After all, he never wrote. He never sent a birthday card. No phone calls. Nothing. Ever.

My eyes went to the painting of me that was still propped against the wall.

Clearly, there *had* been some contact over the years.

Just not to me.

I tried not to let that bother me. Why should it? My father had left to pursue his art. That had nothing to do with me. He'd made his choice long ago. As far as I was concerned, he was dead. It was easier that way.

I dipped my brush in light-blue paint. It was the color of my eyes. The ones I'd inherited from my father. But before I put the brush to the canvas, I let my arm drop and I closed my eyes.

Let it go, Brittany.

When I opened my eyes again, I touched the brush to the blank canvas and swiped the blue across it.

It wasn't anything. But it was *everything*.

Just like that, whatever wall had been built up inside me crumbled to the ground. I made another swipe. And then another. And then...I was painting. And it felt amazing.

For the second time in recent days, I released any of my expectations of what I *should* do and I just let go. Of course, the first time had resulted in the most amazing sex I'd ever experienced, and I had no misconceptions that that same release would result in a masterpiece after decades without picking up a paintbrush. But still, it felt right.

Almost at once, I was completely lost in the work. I let the paintbrush guide my strokes, and time slipped away as I lost myself in the brushstrokes. There hadn't been a plan for my first painting, and when I finally stepped back to assess my work, even I was shocked by what was taking shape in front of me. It was the shoreline of a lake, the mountain peaks just behind it.

Lost Lake.

It had been years since I'd been there, but I'd painted it from memory and I hadn't even realized it.

Some might say that the muse had finally found me again. Or that I had been in some sort of creative trance. In fact, I was sure that Darla would tell me that one really good orgasm had cleared years of pent-up creative tension. The thought of her made me giggle a little. But I was way too practical to actually believe any of that. *Still…*

I put my brush down and grabbed my phone that had been set to silent. I'd left the office early, suddenly feeling the need to paint, and told my assistant, Julie, that I wasn't feeling very good. It had earned exactly the strange look I would expect from her, considering I had only ever called in sick one time in the last three years.

As usual, there were a number of messages in the group text from the girls. I didn't normally join in the chat during the day, choosing work instead. Always.

Until recently.

I stepped backward from my work in progress and typed in a message to the girls.

You'll never believe what I just did!

The moment I sent it, I realized how it might sound. Sure enough, the responses were fast and furious.

Sex.

Crazy hot sex.

Trent!

They weren't wrong, and I laughed as I typed my response.

Well…yes. But guess what else I did?

Again. I should have known better.

Do you mean, who *else?* It was Abby who asked, which was a surprise. I would have expected such a question from Darla.

Not to disappoint, Darla chimed in. *Please tell me it was* who.

This was going to be way easier on video. I abandoned text

messaging and initiated a group video chat. Jessie, Abby, and Darla all hopped on right away. "Where's Sandy?"

Abby shrugged. "Haven't heard from her all day."

"She's been really quiet," Jessie added. "I'll pop over and check on her this evening."

I nodded and made a mental note to reach out to her individually as well. Sandy had a tendency to get quiet from time to time because her two little girls kept her pretty busy. But I worried when she got too quiet. Besides her mother-in-law, we were her main source of support.

"Tell us," Darla demanded. "What or who did you do?" She cackled. "Besides Trent."

"Which," Jessie added quickly, "we want details on, too."

"All the details," Abby said with a firm nod.

I giggled and it was so unexpected that it turned into a full-on laugh. It felt just like we were fifteen again as I told them all about my night with Trent. I still felt mildly guilty for leaving out the details about the agreement we'd made, especially because we only made it because of my little white lie, something I still felt bad about.

"I have to admit," Jessie said when I was done telling them everything—at least, the parts I was comfortable with. "I wasn't sure you were going to go through with it."

"With Trent?"

She nodded. "I don't know why. I just had a strange feeling. But I'm really glad you did, Britt. He's a super hottie and you deserve it."

"It's amazing, isn't it?" Abby said, as if we weren't women in our forties who'd had plenty of sex. "I mean, *this* kind of sex," she added. "The kind when you just let go and don't give a shit. If I'd known how amazing it was, I would have done it a long time ago."

Nobody bothered to mention that she'd been married for

the last fifteen years before she'd divorced her ex and rediscovered her love affair with Phillip.

"Okay, wait," Darla said. "You mentioned that there was something else you did."

"No." I shook my head and turned the screen away from the canvas and my art supplies, suddenly unsure whether I wanted to share this with them. It felt more intimate than I expected it to, and I couldn't figure out why. None of these girls had known me when I was young enough to still have my paints. I'd never mentioned it to them because by the time we'd become close, painting hadn't been part of my life anymore. This would be unexpected. And maybe they'd already had enough of unexpected behavior from me.

Maybe I'd keep this to myself for a little bit longer.

"You know what, I—"

I was cut off by an incoming call.

Trent.

"Girls," I returned quickly to the video, "I have to go. Trent's calling."

I didn't wait for the goodbyes, and no doubt, the teasing laughter that would have followed that announcement before I flipped over to Trent's call.

"Hello."

"Meet me downstairs in ten minutes."

"Hello to you, too." I tried to keep the annoyance out of my voice. We'd barely spoken since the other night, not that we were avoiding each other. In fact, I'd seen him once or twice at the office, but we'd always been busy.

"Hello," he said with the hint of laughter. "Downstairs. Ten minutes. Remember our deal."

The call disconnected, and I stared at my phone for a moment, trying to register what had just happened, and the strange feeling his bossiness had elicited in my belly that there was no mistaking for anything else but desire.

I had my back turned so I didn't see Brittany exit her building exactly eleven minutes later, but I felt her. The air was electrified with an energy I'd only ever felt when she was around and was very quickly beginning to associate with this incredible woman.

"You're late," I said before turning around, and I was glad I did. The moment I laid eyes on her, my breath escaped me, and all the blood shot from my brain to my cock.

Fuck, she was beautiful.

Dressed simply in tailored black pants, a form-fitting white shirt that was likely cashmere or something else equally expensive, and a matching black jacket, she looked both casual and elegant.

"You were timing me?"

I couldn't take my eyes off those red lips. I loved that she'd freshly applied her lipstick for me. Unless, of course, she just sat around the house looking this put together, which was equally plausible.

"I told you ten minutes."

"The elevator was slow."

Damn, I loved her spark. It wasn't hard to see how much she loved me bossing her around a little bit. Hell, Brittany had probably never had a man dare to attempt to take charge the way I had done so easily. It turned her on. That particular feeling was very, *very* mutual. But just as much as I enjoyed it, I equally enjoyed the way she pushed back. Just a little. Enough to let me know the only reason I was telling her what to do was because she was allowing it.

Fuck, but the woman was magnificent.

Which was exactly why I'd done my best to keep my distance for the last few days after our little back-alley fuck. Brittany was dangerous. It wasn't hard to see that she could very quickly become addictive. Hell, already she was literally all I could think of.

And that's the entire reason I stood here now.

"Come," I said. "We're going to be late." I turned and started walking, tucking my hand into my slacks instead of reaching for hers, which was what I really wanted to do.

I held the door for her, and Brittany slipped into the front seat of my BMW.

It wasn't until I was seated next to her and driving away that she asked, "And where are we headed on a Wednesday afternoon? Shouldn't you be at work?"

I glanced in her direction. "Shouldn't you?"

"I wasn't feeling well."

"You look perfectly fine to me." I shook my head. "No," I corrected myself. "You look fantastic, Brittany. You always do."

"A compliment?" She tossed her head back and laughed.

But I wasn't laughing. "Haven't I done that before?" The question was genuine. "Really? Have I never given you a compliment?"

Her laughter died at my serious tone. "Honestly?"

I nodded.

"You might have," she said. "I don't really hear compliments."

"You don't *hear* them?"

She shook her head. "Not usually. And honestly, it's not that I don't think I'm worthy of them. It's really not a self-esteem thing."

I believed that.

"It's just, I never really heard any growing up, so I think I've kind of trained myself not to notice if I was or wasn't getting them."

"That's the most horrible thing I've ever heard." I took my eyes off the road just long enough to see her blush, but only a little before it was gone again. "Get ready, Brittany, you magnificent creature. I'm going to give you so many compliments that you have no choice but to start hearing them. Okay?"

She laughed again.

It was a fabulous sound, and I wanted to hear a whole lot more of it.

"Are you going to tell me where we're going?"

"I don't have to." I pulled my car into the parking lot. "We're here."

I was watching, so I didn't miss when the look of surprise registered on her face. "The Pines? This is a nursing home." Brittany turned to me. "What are we doing here?"

"The term *seniors'* home is preferred, actually. And I volunteer here."

"You volunteer here?"

I nodded, enjoying her shock. It was fun to keep her guessing. "A few times a week, actually. There's a lot you don't know about me, Brittany." I winked, and she laughed.

"I believe that," she said. "And I have to tell you, you surprise me, Trent. I never would have guessed that this is where we were going. Not in a million years. Not after…"

I reached for her and put my hand on her thigh. "Not to worry, baby. There will be more of that later." Her eyes flashed, darkening the way that I loved to see. "Plenty more." I squeezed her thigh a little and let my finger wander toward the cleft of her legs. "After all, we have to give you something to tell your friends, right? That was the deal."

Brittany swallowed hard, betraying the sense of control she was trying to convey. "We do."

"And we will." I patted her leg once before withdrawing. She wasn't the only one trying to stay in control. "But first, we have some seniors to help. And today is Bingo."

I went around to her car door and held it open for her as she stepped out to stand in front of me. I knew I was playing with fire, having her so close in such a public place. A public place where people *knew* me, and I had a certain reputation. But it didn't matter. Not at that moment because those red lips were begging to have mine on them.

I slipped my hand through her silky hair and cupped her head as I pulled her in for a kiss.

It wasn't long—I was only human, after all—but it was enough to stoke the fires. And they were thoroughly and properly stoked when I pulled back.

"Your lipstick..." For the first time, I noticed that it hadn't smudged at all. "It's..."

She pulled out a compact from her purse, did a quick check and, satisfied, snapped it shut before putting it back in her purse. "Stays put through pretty much anything. Pretty impressive, right?"

"It's not the only thing." The compliment came easy.

"So," Brittany deflected. "Bingo, huh?"

"Sure is." I took her hand in mine as we walked toward the door. "Oh." I stopped her before we stepped up to the sliding doors. "One more thing when we go in there."

Brittany waited.

I squeezed her hand and gave her my most charming smile. "As far as anyone is concerned, you're my girlfriend."

Chapter Nine

OH, this was interesting.

Girlfriend.

Nowhere in our deal was there any mention of that.

I tried to catch Trent's eye again as we walked through the doors, but he steadfastly looked forward, so I squeezed his hand a little bit instead. That did it. He glanced over at me and gave me a wry grin. Moments later, I saw a completely different version of Trent Thomas than I could have ever expected.

He moved smoothly through the lobby of the building, stopped to say hi to various residents, flirt a little with the ladies and talks sports scores with the men. I didn't even know Trent followed sports.

Not once did he fail to introduce me. As his girlfriend.

It felt strange, but only at first. Maybe we were both good actors, but it didn't take long for me to completely embrace the role of devoted girlfriend. I held his hand, laughed when it was appropriate and teased him, even when it wasn't.

Trent was just as smooth. He kissed my cheek more times than I could count and complimented me in front of almost everyone we met. He hadn't been lying when he said he was going to make that a priority.

It was true what I'd said, too. I hardly ever noticed a compliment. But something about the way Trent gave them...I listened.

"Well, here you both are," Trent said as we came to a couple at the table off to the side, in front of the window. We'd already been around the entire room, and I got the impression that Trent had been saving these two for last.

"Florence? Roy? I'd like you to meet Brittany. My *girlfriend*."

With the emphasis he put on the last word, I understood immediately that these two were the entire reason I was there.

Playing my role perfectly, I extended my hand. "It's nice to meet you—"

"Nonsense," Florence said sharply.

I glanced back at Trent. *Did they not believe him?*

"I will only accept a hug from the woman who has captured the heart of our Trent." She reached out her arms.

Relieved and also completely smitten with her, I bent down to receive what was a shockingly strong hug before turning to Roy.

"Quite a looker, aren't you?" He crooked a finger toward me. I moved to give him a hug as well, but before he let go, he took my hand and placed a slight kiss on the top. "We sure are pleased to meet you, Brittany."

"I told you I had a girlfriend," Trent said with a twinge of pride in his voice. "You didn't think I could land someone as beautiful as her, did you?" He held out a chair for me, before taking one himself.

"Oh, Trent." Florence slapped his arm playfully. "I didn't doubt you for a minute."

"Not true," her husband interjected. "I believe she was arranging your blind date earlier this morning."

My eyes open wide, I looked to Trent, who shrugged.

"I told them there was no point. I was already spoken for."

I knew it was only pretend. Hell, it had been *my* idea, after all. Still, something about the way he said that gave me flutters in my stomach.

"He appears to be," the older woman said with a sly smile. "Now, Brittany. Tell me about yourself."

I spent the next few minutes giving them the abridged bio of my career and life while Trent sat next to me, his arm casually draped over my shoulders. A fact I was very aware of. Maybe I should have been concerned about how much Trent affected me with only the slightest touch. After all, this wasn't real and it certainly wasn't going to last.

"Tell me how you all have become so close," I asked when I was done with my brief introduction. "Trent really hasn't told me much about his time volunteering here." I gave Trent a quick glance.

"Is that right?" Roy said. "He certainly hasn't told us much about you either, my dear."

"I'm a very private person," Trent said. "Besides, it's good to have a few secrets."

I tipped my head and eyed him. "Is it?"

Trent squeezed my shoulders tighter. "It is. And to answer your question, I got to know Roy and Flo here the first day I started volunteering. They kind of adopted me."

"We sure did, and it was one of our best decisions ever." Flo's smile lit up her face.

"*One* of," Roy said, his eyes filled with love and adoration for his wife. "But not even close to my *best* decision." He leaned over and kissed her cheek tenderly.

It was probably the sweetest thing I'd ever seen, and my heart clenched a little in my chest. I couldn't even begin to understand what it would be like to have that kind of love. The kind that lasted for decades, through hard times and good. Only growing stronger with each day.

What would that feel like to have someone love me in that way? For the first time…ever…I was envious of love. My chest felt tight and suddenly I needed air.

"What was this about Bingo today?"

Trent glanced over in my direction and mercifully noticed I needed a break. "Right." He jumped to his feet. "It's got to be almost time for Bingo, and I don't want to shirk my duties." He laughed easily. "Today I'm going to get Brittany to read out the numbers," he continued. "I have a feeling our male residents might like that a bit more than staring at my ugly mug."

"It was so nice to meet you both," I said genuinely as I stood next to Trent.

"We do hope to see you again soon, dear."

"Don't keep her away from us, Trent. She's far too pretty to keep hidden."

I blushed and when Trent slipped his arm around my waist and held me close, for the briefest of moments, it all felt real.

And I liked it. A lot.

I don't think I'd ever had a bad day volunteering at the Pines. But none of those days came even close to how much I'd enjoyed my time with Brittany, handing out cards and daubers and pulling Bingo balls.

She'd gone with the flow so easily, laughing and teasing with both the residents and myself, there was more than one instance when I forgot it wasn't real. She wasn't *really* my girl-friend. We weren't really a couple. We were fucking. That was it.

It was crass. Even to think it. But it was the distinction I needed in order to keep myself in check. Nothing good would come of it if I let myself think, even for a moment, that what we were doing was anything more than a deal.

"You were a natural in there," I said once we were back in my car.

"Are you surprised?" She tossed her hair over her shoulder, leaving her neck exposed.

Damn, I wanted to pull the car over right there on the highway and kiss that delicate skin. My cock thickened in my pants just thinking about the moans she'd make as I nibbled my way down the length of her neck.

I pulled my attention back to the road. "No," I said. "I mean, pretty much everything about you surprises me, therefore nothing does."

"That doesn't make sense." She laughed again.

It was like music. To think I'd never heard it only a few days ago and now it was one of my favorite *songs*. Second only to the cries she made when she was coming. Hard.

"I have to tell you, Trent. You know what *was* surprising?"

I shook my head. "Tell me."

"You. The Pines. I think it's the last thing I expected from you. You don't seem like the type."

I knew that was coming. There was a reason I didn't tell anyone about my volunteering.

"What type is that?"

"The tough guy, super-slick businessman who doesn't give a fuck about anyone or anything as long as he gets the deal."

That stung, but I shouldn't have been surprised after what had happened with her friend Jessie and her diner. *Still.* I thought we'd moved past that.

"That's still how you think of me?"

She hesitated, so I glanced in her direction. She was looking at her lap, her hands twisted together.

"Brittany?"

"No," she said quietly and looked up to meet my eyes.

There was a softness in her gaze I'd never seen before. It sucked me in. I could have lost myself all day in her eyes.

Thankfully, a moment later, a pothole reminded me that I was still behind the wheel of the car and although I may *want* to look into those glacial-blue eyes all day, I also didn't want to get us killed.

"I don't think of you that way anymore," she continued. "I'm actually...well, I'm not actually sure how to think about you."

Before I could respond to the thought, she chuckled and the seriousness of the moment was gone. "But you have to tell me how you ended up volunteering at a seniors' home, of all places. Don't tell me you were trying to soften them up so you could buy the land."

"What? You don't think I'd—" I cut off when I saw the grin on her face. "You're just screwing with me."

"Of course."

Her sass was sexy, if not infuriating at times.

"But seriously."

"Seriously?"

She nodded.

"I was raised by my grandparents. My parents died when I was young. So I guess I've always felt a special connection to elderly people," I confessed. "They've lived full and rich lives. They've seen and experienced things we could only dream about. And the terrible thing is that society just kind of discards them and their history, as if when you get old you aren't valuable anymore. I hate that." I kept my eyes on the road as I spoke. "My grandparents were everything to me. And ever since they passed, I've felt a hole in my life. It's hard to explain but the connection you have with your grandparents is different from anything else, you know?"

I looked at Brittany. The smile had vanished from her face, her pretty red lips pressed into a tight line. "I don't know."

"You don't have grandparents?"

"You don't have parents."

"Touché." I nodded.

"To be fair," Brittany added a moment later, "I don't have parents either."

Now, that was a surprise. "I'm sorry to hear that."

"I'm not."

There was no way I could hide my shock at that one. "Care to elaborate?"

"Not really." She turned and faced out the window, shutting down further conversation on the matter.

We drove in silence for a few minutes before she spoke again. "My mom died a few months ago. We weren't close. Ever. I haven't seen my dad since I was a kid," she added. "But..."

I waited.

"I just learned that he might have seen me."

She still didn't turn away from the window. There was so much sadness in her voice that I yearned to reach out to her, but something told me that would close her off, so I fought the urge.

"I think that's the part that hurts the most," Brittany added. She inhaled deeply and turned to me on the exhale. "And it does hurt." She swallowed hard. "I've never told anyone that," she said. "I mean, my friends know that my dad has been out of the picture for a while, but…"

"Thank you for trusting me." I reached for her hand then. "I'm sorry I brought it up. I didn't—"

"No." She squeezed my hand. "I think I actually needed to talk about it more than I thought."

It wasn't lost on me that we hadn't actually done much talking on the matter, but it was a start. And maybe that's all she needed.

Chapter Ten

I WASN'T a touchy-feely kind of person, but that didn't mean that I didn't feel deeply. I did. I just didn't like to talk about those feelings, ever. Which was why I was so surprised that the words came out so easily with Trent. He didn't know me. Not really. He didn't have any preconceived notion of who I was, or where I came from. There was an ease in sharing with someone who hadn't known you your whole life.

Equally surprising was how good it had felt to tell him the little bit that I had. It wasn't much, and I certainly hadn't gone into any details. But it was a start. And despite what my mother had led me to believe, the earth wouldn't explode if I dared to share our *personal* life with anyone.

"Our business is *our* business, Brittany," she'd said when I was only thirteen and she'd overheard me telling my friends that I spent my evenings alone because my mom was usually working. "Nothing good ever came from sharing your personal dramas with outsiders."

"But they're my friends."

"They're outsiders to our family," she said coldly. "Do you

know what happens when the wrong people hear stories that aren't true?"

"But it is true."

That earned me a slap across the face. I knew better than to cry out but my eyes watered with tears I struggled to hold back as she continued her lecture.

"Nothing good will come from outsiders knowing our business. It's drama we don't need. And that's all it is when you talk like that. Drama. Rise above the gossip and useless conversation, and keep your bloody mouth shut."

The memory still stung. I hadn't thought about that moment in a very long time, but I remembered it vividly, and obviously, my subconscious had also never forgotten. There was a reason I didn't share much.

"You look like you're lost in thought."

Jerked from my memory, I looked back to Trent. We'd fallen into silence, and I hadn't even noticed that he'd taken a different road home. "Where are we going?" I changed the subject altogether. "This isn't the way to my apartment."

His smile was wicked and instantly cleared my mind from any and all thoughts that didn't involve those lips on mine.

"I never said I was taking you home." He wiggled his eyebrows. "You didn't think that was all we were doing today, did you?"

I shrugged, and he laughed.

"Oh, baby. I'm far from done with you."

His voice held a promise that I felt directly between my legs. It had been less than a week since our first hook-up, but it was already way too long.

"Besides," Trent added, "I have something to show you."

A few minutes later, we pulled up to the valet station at the Empress, the fanciest hotel in town.

"Is this where you're staying?"

"For now."

We slipped from his sporty car, and Trent draped his arm around my waist easily, as if it were the most natural thing in the world. I fought the urge to lean into his touch and held myself tall as we walked through the lobby. There was a good chance we'd see someone we knew, and I wasn't sure how I felt about that. Did I want people to know I was with Trent when it wasn't anything more than a temporary arrangement? People would talk. There would be gossip, and—*fuck it.*

I was forty-one, for goodness' sake. Why did I still give a shit what other people thought or said about me and what I may or may not be doing? Particularly considering they didn't have the facts?

I didn't.

At least, I was going to try very, very hard not to.

Trent tightened his grip on me, and I chose that moment to prove to myself that I didn't care about what anyone thought. I stopped walking, pulling him to a stop as well in the middle of the opulent lobby.

"What are you—"

I spun my body into his and pressed myself up against him. Trent's arms came around me, naturally holding me tight as I lifted my head to kiss him. Right there in front of anyone who might be watching. There was no doubt in my mind that tongues would be wagging.

"What was that?" He narrowed his eyes in suspicion. "I don't take you for a public display of affection kind of woman."

"You don't think so?" I challenged.

Trent didn't speak for a moment, but soon his lips twisted up into a grin. "Well," he said. "If that's the case…"

He moved so quickly, taking my hand and pulling me along toward the elevator, that I had to work not to stumble to keep up. We stood in silence, his hand gripping mine tightly as we waited for the elevator to arrive. But the moment we were inside and the door shut behind us, Trent pulled me hard up against him. He held my face as he kissed me thoroughly while his free hand skimmed the side of my body. Desire shot through me; my panties were instantly damp between my legs.

"If you like public displays…"

I'd been in the hotel enough times to know that after the fourth floor, the glass on three sides of the elevator opened up with a view of the mountains, the town, and the street below.

Trent reached behind him and pushed the button for the penthouse before spinning me around and pressing me against the glass. The elevator shot upward as Trent's hands made quick work of the button on my slacks and pushed them down over my ass.

"What are you—"

"Ssh." He flipped my hair off my neck and murmured in my ear. "You said you liked public displays of affection."

What? No! Not here.

My mind raced. *There was no way. He wasn't going to fuck me in the elevator. Not where anyone could—* The elevator came to a jarring halt beneath me.

"I think here's good," Trent said.

I could hear the amusement in his voice. He *did* plan on fucking me in the elevator.

We were about five or six stories up from the ground. High enough that unless someone purposely looked up, they wouldn't notice what was going on inside the elevator. But low enough that *if* they did look up, they would be able to see and know exactly what was going on. Clearly.

"Trent, what the—"

He quieted me again by biting down, just a little, on my neck. "Listen, remember?"

"But this is—"

"So fucking hot," he finished for me. And he wasn't wrong.

My clit was throbbing for him. Knowing that someone

might be able to see us *was* incredibly hot. Never mind that having Trent's cock inside me again had been almost an all-consuming thought for the last few days.

In response, I pushed my ass back against him.

He growled in response. "Hands against the glass."

I did as I was told.

"Don't move."

I didn't plan on it. Still, I wriggled my ass again in defiance. His growl, followed by a sharp, stinging smack against my lace-clad butt cheek, sent another wave of need through me. My panties would be completely ruined by now.

Behind me, I could hear the zipper of his pants, followed by the tearing of a foil packet, and then Trent's hard cock was pressed up against me.

Reflexively, I pushed my bottom out to give him better access.

He folded over me to kiss my neck again and whisper in my ear. "Have you ever fucked on an elevator before?"

I knew he already knew the answer. Still, I said, "You're my first."

"Umm. I like that." His hand slipped between my legs. "And I like how fucking wet you are for it. For me."

It was my turn to groan when he slipped a finger inside me and wiggled it before pinching my sensitive nub as he withdrew.

"Keep your eyes open," he ordered. "The whole time. No matter what. Understand?"

I nodded.

"Good girl." He thrust inside me.

Instinctively, my eyes shut as he filled me. "Fuck." The word was little more than a groan that slipped from my lips. He was so big, and I should have expected it, been ready for it. But I wasn't prepared for the rush of sensations that crashed through me.

"Open your eyes," he commanded as he thrust into me again. Hard.

How did he—

"Look down," he said, forcing me out of my head and back into the moment. "Look at all the people down there who could see you at any moment."

I did as he instructed and scanned the street below for the first time. To my horror and equal thrill, we were much lower than I'd initially thought. We were close enough to the ground that there would be no denying what it was we were doing.

Trent thrust into me again from behind, pressing me hard into the glass. I braced myself against him, wanting all of him.

"God, you're sexy, Brittany." He sucked and nipped on my neck a little as he increased the pace of his thrusts.

He felt so good inside me, but I knew we didn't have long. We were only seconds away from getting caught. Any moment, someone could look up and—*shit.*

Trent saw it at the same time I did. A casually dressed man, likely a tourist, looked up and made direct eye contact with me. Terror flashed through me, and I stiffened.

"He sees you," Trent whispered into my ear. He reached around and passed a finger to my clit, sending a wave of heat to my pussy. "He sees me fucking you, doesn't he?"

I nodded. As much as I wanted to close my eyes so I couldn't see the man watching us, I kept them open, equally turned on knowing he could see us.

"He's going to watch you come," Trent said next. "Do you like that?"

I didn't answer immediately, and Trent nipped the tender skin on my neck, prodding a response from me.

"I do," I answered honestly. "I do like that he's watching."

"I thought you might." Trent thrust hard into me at the same moment that he pinched my clit between his fingers, sending me straight into a dazzling climax. I bit my bottom lip to keep from crying out, but hot tears pricked at my eyes from the intensity of my orgasm.

Behind me, I vaguely noticed as Trent stiffened and took his own release.

A moment later, he pulled out of me. My hands still pressed against the glass, more for the support my legs were not providing me. I struggled to control my breathing.

"Fuck, baby. That was insane." Trent pulled up my pants and wrapped his arms around me as he buttoned them for me. "Blow him a kiss," he ordered. "After all, you have him to thank for that."

I didn't completely agree with that. My vision cleared enough to bring our spectator back into focus. I stepped back from the window and did as Trent told me, blowing a kiss, before turning to face Trent.

The moment he did, he hit the button to resume our elevator trip and pulled me in for a kiss.

"You're full of surprises, Brittany. In all the best ways."

There was no way I thought she'd go along with the whole elevator thing. But she did. And it was without a doubt the hottest sex I'd *ever* had. No comparison.

Not. Even. Close.

The elevator came to a stop. I took her hand and led her into the penthouse I was renting until I could find something more permanent. My trip to Aspen Valley had started as a temporary business trip to investigate the opportunity for development for my company. It hadn't taken long for me to see the potential in business. And I was just as quickly starting to see that same potential in other areas as well.

Brittany was still a little shaky from her orgasm, so I led her straight to the couch. "Can I get you a drink? Water? Or maybe—"

"A vodka soda would be great." She looked up at me. "I think the situation calls for one, don't you?"

There was no way to keep the grin off my face. "Absolutely."

When I returned a few minutes later with our drinks, she seemed to have made a full recovery.

"Thank you." Brittany accepted her drink and took a sip. "I don't usually drink in the middle of the afternoon," she said. "To be honest, I don't usually drink much at all."

This much I knew.

"But then again, I don't usually have voyeuristic sex in an elevator either."

"Not usually?" I sat next to her on the couch, but facing her so our knees touched. More and more, I wanted to be touching her in some way.

"Okay," Brittany admitted. "I've never had sex on an elevator before. And I've also never had sex when others are watching."

I chuckled. "You know you gave that guy images to last him a lifetime of lonely showers, right?"

She almost choked on her drink, but she laughed, too. "I'm not sure I want to think about that." She shook her head. "Besides, he's not the only one who's going to have images to last a lifetime."

She mumbled the last part to herself, but I caught it clearly.

I put my drink on the coffee table and slipped my hand up her thigh. I squeezed gently until she looked at me. There was no mistaking the flicker of sadness I saw there, and after what we'd just done, I couldn't even begin to understand what could possibly be making her sad.

Determined to put a smile back on her face, I asked, "Did you text your friends about that one yet?"

Maybe I should have been upset that she was using me to give her friends stories about wild sexual exploits, but I didn't care. No, that wasn't true. I *liked* it. Knowing that Brittany was going to share our experiences with her friends fueled me to be better and more exciting. Not that I needed a whole lot of inspiration when it came to Brittany. Everything about her inspired me. In every way.

"I didn't yet," she said. "I mean...I've barely even recovered."

I loved her vulnerability with me.

"I wasn't sure I would have been able to walk on my own after that," she said. "I have never come so hard in my life."

My cock twitched to life at her words and the knowledge that *I* had done that to her. *For* her. It was a huge turn-on.

I leaned over and pressed my lips to hers in a soft kiss. "I'm glad. You deserve to come hard like that every time."

She laughed. "I'm not sure I could survive it. Really."

I was pretty sure she could. And dammed if I didn't want to make sure she came that hard every single time for the rest of her life. Instead of saying it out loud, which I knew wouldn't result in anything good, I kissed her again before sitting back and once more picking up my drink.

"It doesn't bother you that I'm telling my friends all the dirty details?" Brittany eyed me over the rim of her glass. "I mean, a lot of men wouldn't like that at all."

"I don't know what type of men you hang out with, baby. But as far as I'm concerned, having my woman tell her girl-friends about all of the earth-shattering, can hardly walk after-ward, crazy orgasms I'm giving her is hardly a problem."

Her eyes widened, and I realized my slip.

"Your woman?"

"I just meant that...well..."

Fuck it.

I grabbed her hand and tugged her closer to me. "Yes." I

committed to it. "My woman. For the next few weeks, for longer. For…it doesn't matter. But as long as I'm the one making you scream like that, then *yes* you're my woman." I kissed her again. Harder this time, to make my point. "Got it?"

She swallowed hard and her lips flicked up into a small smile. "Oh," she said slowly. "I got it."

Damn, she was going to be hard to walk away from. And for the life of me, it was getting harder and harder to remember exactly why I might want to.

Fortunately, Brittany's phone rang, forcing me to pull away from her and the moment.

"Sorry," she said. "I should check, since…well, it is a workday."

"You don't have to explain it to me." I took the opportunity to cross the room and check my own phone for messages. I had a real estate agent looking into appropriate office spaces. I'd made the decision to stay in Aspen Valley, at least for a little while, so I was going to need to lease some office space. The head office for Thomas Developments would still be based out east, but I liked the idea of a satellite office more and more. Especially considering there was so much opportunity. I'd need somewhere for my staff to be, and as generous as Shane Grant had been with his space, it was time to move on.

I scrolled through a few messages about potential properties but got distracted a moment later when Brittany put her call on speakerphone.

It was her friend, Jessie.

"Remember the other night, we were talking about a dinner party at our place, and you agreed to come?"

My messages forgotten, I turned and leaned back against the kitchen island, suddenly far more interested in Brittany's response.

She glanced my way as she said, "I remember. When are you thinking?"

"Friday."

"*This* Friday?"

"You have plans?"

Brittany looked directly at me, but I could only laugh. I would happily fill every minute of her calendar and tie her to my bed for the duration of the four weeks if I thought I could get away with it.

Actually, that didn't sound like a bad idea at all.

"I don't have plans," she said to Jessie, her gaze still on mine.

"You do now," Jessie said. "And of course, Trent's invited, too. Now that you're together, you can—"

"We're not together."

Brittany dropped her gaze and something in my chest twisted, which was dumb. It was just sex. That's all it was ever going to be. That was the agreement. And even if it wasn't, I didn't want anything more. I *never* wanted anything more. Why should this time be different?

But it didn't matter why it should, or if it would, because I already knew the truth. This time *was* different.

Chapter Eleven

JESSIE AND SHANE'S new home was gorgeous. It was beyond gorgeous, really, and I couldn't be happier for my friend. She'd spent her whole life working harder than almost anyone else I knew to raise her twins and keep her diner afloat after her no-good ex-husband basically left her with nothing. Not that his leaving was a real loss. Barrett had always been a loser. Still, it hadn't been easy for Jessie, and it made me happier than I could express to see her thriving now that she and Shane had found each other.

"This house is incredible, Jessie." I hugged her tight and handed her the bottle of wine I'd brought.

"Thank you. I can't believe you haven't been here yet."

I could. I'd been so busy working. As usual, work had consumed all of my time. Until lately. More and more, I was reconsidering my workaholic ways. Maybe I'd been wrong all these years about the value of putting work first.

"Where's Trent?" Jessie's question jerked me from my thoughts. "Didn't you come together?"

I stiffened. "Why would we do that?"

I knew exactly *why* we would do that. And that's exactly why I'd insisted that we didn't. Every time I spent time with Trent, it felt a little easier. A little *better*. And it wasn't just the sex, although that was also getting better and better, if it were even possible. But it was more than that, and that scared the hell out of me. Nothing about what we were doing supposed to be serious, and it was definitely not supposed to be permanent. Exactly the opposite, in fact.

Jessie tilted her head and narrowed her eyes at me. "I thought you guys were together?"

"Who's together?" Abby and Sandy entered the kitchen. There was a flurry of hugs and greetings before Abby returned to the question, much to my disappointment. "So," she said. "Who's together?"

"Trent and Brittany."

"I told you." I stopped Jessie. "We're *not* together."

"You're not?" Sandy looked taken aback. "Did you not just tell us about some crazy-hot sex in an elevator? I mean, I don't even know if I'll be able to look him in the eyes after hearing that story." She blushed, and I looked to Abby for support.

"It's just sex," I said. "You said it yourself, right?"

Abby's face was carefully neutral.

"Just go have fun, let go a little and…casual, right?"

"I don't know if I said that."

I wanted to scream with frustration, but the girls laughed.

"Sorry," Jessie said. "I honestly did think you guys were together. I mean, you're sure spending a lot of time together."

"We're having a lot of super-hot sex," I fired back. "That's it. There's nothing else going on."

I made my point and swallowed hard, because even as I said it, it didn't feel right. There was no way I was going to admit it, at least not out loud, but there was something else going on with Trent and me. Something I didn't fully understand, and it definitely wasn't something I'd ever experienced. It was a closeness I'd only ever had with my girlfriends before. But with Trent, it was different because, well…because not only was I telling him things I hadn't told anyone—including my closest friends—but we were also having sex and…well, there was something else, but I couldn't quite put my finger on it, so it was easier to pretend it was nothing.

"Well," Jessie said, her voice full of cheer. "Trent did RSVP, so I'm sure we'll see him later."

She led us through the house, pointing out a few details to me because the others had been there numerous times already. A detail I felt guiltier and guiltier about. I really did have to make a change when it came to work-life balance.

"There they are," Jessie called out when we finally got through to the large living room. Shane, Phillip, a man I'd never met before, and Trent stood together along the bar. "I was just wondering if you all were hiding from us."

Shane immediately crossed the room to her, pulled her close, and kissed her in front of everyone. "Never, my love."

Something in my stomach flipped to see them together. So easily and completely in love.

Was I jealous? *No.* I had never in my life been jealous about a relationship. *Never.*

I tried not to, but my eyes moved on their own accord to look at Trent, who stared directly at me with a small knowing smile on his own face. I shook my head and glanced away, as he started to walk across the room toward me.

"Hey, baby." He wrapped his arm around me and kissed me on the lips.

In front of everyone.

So much for convincing my friends we weren't together.

Sure enough, I caught Abby's eye, and she laughed.

Trent squeezed me tight once more before releasing me and turning to my friends. "Abby, hi. And Jessie, nice to see you again. And you must be Sandy," he said smoothly as he took my friend's hand. "We haven't officially met." He took her hand and kissed the back of it while completely unexpected and unfamiliar jealousy burned through me.

What the hell was that?

Sandy looked at me, an expression that looked very much like a question on her face. I shrugged in an effort to look indifferent.

Trent, his hand still on Sandy's, looked at me with a grin. "Doesn't Brittany look stunning today?"

Another compliment. True to his word, he never did miss an opportunity.

A series of responses ran through my head before rejecting them until finally, Trent said, "A simple thank-you will do."

He smiled broadly, and I both simultaneously wanted to kill him and kiss him at that moment.

Before I got the chance, he turned his attention back to Sandy. "Have you met Dylan yet? Let me introduce you," he added when she didn't respond. Trent looked over his shoulder and said, "Grab me a drink and meet me on the patio in five."

Seriously?

He was going to boss me around in front of my friends?

Oh, he was pushing the limits of our deal and judging by his wink, he knew it.

Still.

Okay, so telling her to get me a drink was probably a step too far, particularly given the look on her face. But it was fun to push her limits, and it would be equally hot later when I pushed them even further. Besides, if she was a little bit upset, I'd more than make it up to her.

"Dylan, have you met Sandy yet?"

I did my duty and made the introduction, which really wasn't my duty at all considering I was not the host of this event, and rumor had it, Shane had invited his old friend, Dylan, whom I'd only met a handful of times, in an effort to set him up with Jessie's friend Darla. Who wasn't even in attendance. Truth be told, I was probably going against all social etiquette, but I didn't care.

Trying for inconspicuous, I scanned the room as I made the introduction. Brittany was nowhere to be found.

"Dylan here owns one of the largest ranching organizations for miles," I continued. "Do you like horses, Sandy?" I was pretty sure it was a stupid question, but her eyes lit up and she leaned in toward Dylan.

I hadn't been properly introduced to their friend Darla, either. But judging by the way these two had fallen into easy conversation, already forgetting I was there, they seemed like the better match if one was to be made.

They didn't notice when I slipped away to search for my woman.

I found her on the patio. With two drinks. I approached her cautiously.

"I'm not your servant." She all but spat the words out at me when I was close enough. Her eyes had darkened; she was fired up, but I was pretty sure she wasn't going to throw the drink at me. At least, I hoped not.

I stood directly in front of her, our mouths only inches apart. "No, you are most definitely *not* my servant." I ran a finger down her cheek, my cock twitching to life when she closed her eyes and inhaled softly. "But you did promise to listen to me."

Brittany's eyes snapped open. "In the bedroom, not in—"

I silenced her with a kiss. The small moan that slipped from her mouth into mine told me everything I needed to know.

When I pulled away, I kept my arm wrapped tightly around her waist, holding her close.

"You didn't seem happy to see me."

"I'm always happy to see you."

The words shocked and thrilled me. They'd obviously surprised her, too. Brittany immediately pressed her lips together in a line.

"You are, are you?" I teased. I was certain she was going to deny it, but she didn't.

"I actually am."

Her face was full of sincerity and a vulnerability I'd never seen in her before.

She chuckled. "I probably shouldn't have said that. But what the hell?"

What the hell indeed?

Something inside me warmed, and for the first time with Brittany, it wasn't purely sexual. Okay, maybe it wasn't the first time. But it was the first time I recognized it for what it was. I liked her. I genuinely liked her in a way I'd never liked any other woman.

I was also always happy to see her. It hadn't been long since we'd started this whole…whatever it was we were doing. But did that matter? Was there supposed to be a timeline on how I was supposed to feel at certain times? Who gave a fuck if there was?

"Brittany, I—"

"Hey, you guys!" Shane's voice interrupted our private moment. "Time to eat," Shane called. "Grab a drink and get to the table."

We did as we were told, taking our drinks with us as we joined the others. Before we'd even sat down, Brittany had downed her drink. In fact, as the evening progressed, Brittany, who hardly ever drank alcohol, always seemed to have a drink in her hand. She didn't appear drunk, but if she kept going, it wouldn't be long before she did or said something I knew she'd regret in the morning.

Dinner was barely over when I took Brittany's hand, stood and announced we would be leaving early. It probably went against all kinds of social conventions, and no doubt I'd hear about it from Shane later, but I didn't care. I knew Brittany well enough to know that something was going on with her. There was no other explanation for why she would be drinking so excessively in the situation.

She didn't resist when I insisted on leaving her car behind and taking mine, and it wasn't until we pulled up at the valet of her building that she said, "We probably shouldn't have left so early."

"Are you upset?"

She shook her head. "No. I…well…thanks for driving me home."

Yes. Something was definitely going on. Her behavior had changed so quickly. Right after she'd admitted to being happy to see me. *But why?* I grabbed her hand. "I'll walk you up."

Her eyes flared with the promise of more, but for the first time ever, I wasn't interested in fucking her. Not if she was drunk.

I'd never been up to Brittany's top-floor condo. Immediately upon setting foot into the room, I was impressed. It was beautiful. Tastefully furnished in clean lines. Everything white and light gray, with blue accents that matched her eyes. Professional, crisp and modern. It reminded me of Brittany, but it was missing something.

Britt came off as slick and cold. *Ice Queen*, I used to think of her as. And this living space matched that. But the more I got to know, the more I could see there was more to Brittany than initially met the eye. There was a warmth to her that this space didn't convey at all.

She walked straight through into the living room, expecting me to follow. Which I did.

"What's this?"

I stopped short at two paintings that were propped up in the hallway.

"Nothing," she called from the kitchen. "Just some garbage I need to take out. Want a drink?"

"Not even a little," I called before turning my attention back to the paintings. They were good. *Really* good. And they were portraits of Brittany. One as a young girl, and one where she was a bit older. A young woman. They were both stunning and…haunting.

In the living room was an easel with a painting of mountains propped up on it. On the floor next to the easel was a small stack of other paintings as well. I had no idea Brittany was an artist.

Always full of surprises.

"Britt?" I went in search of her and found her sitting on the white marble kitchen island, another drink in her hand. I stood in front of her and took the drink gently out of her hand. "Want to talk about it?"

She shook her head. "I think I did enough talking earlier, don't you?"

Oh.

"Is that what this is all about?" I held her head still and forced her to look at me when I said what I should have said much earlier. "I'm always happy to see you, too."

It wasn't a lie. Or some sort of bullshit I was saying because I thought it was what she wanted to hear. Not even close.

"You're just saying that so I don't feel stupid."

"Do I look like the type of man to say something I don't mean?"

Reluctantly, she shook her head.

I kissed her softly. "Just like you're not the type of woman to say what you don't mean."

She thought about it for a minute. "It still doesn't mean anything. Four weeks. That's it."

"Whatever you say." I kissed her again, purposely not mentioning the extension clause that I was thinking about more and more. "It's early. How about some coffee?"

Chapter Twelve

THERE WAS a reason I never drank. And after two very strong black coffees, I remembered exactly what that reason was.

I lost control. A little bit of alcohol in my system, and I started saying things I didn't mean, or worse—things I *did* mean and had no business saying.

I took a good long look at myself in the mirror, and my face burned at the memory of what I'd said to Trent.

I'm always happy to see you.

I mean, seriously? Who actually said things like that? I was mortified. All I really wanted to do was change into my pajamas and crawl into bed with Sheldon, who'd been in hiding ever since we'd come home. He didn't usually like it when I brought strangers into my apartment. He wasn't likely to make an appearance until Trent left.

Which didn't seem to be anytime soon. In fact, he looked quite comfortable on the couch, one leg crossed over the other, his arms tucked behind his head when I returned from the bathroom. No. He didn't look like he was going anywhere soon.

With a sigh, I sank down into the oversized chair across

from him and picked up my glass of water that I'd switched to, having had enough of the coffee.

"Feeling better?"

"I wasn't feeling bad," I shot back.

He was clearly trying hard not to laugh. "Right."

"Do you think it's funny?"

"Yes."

My spine stiffened, but as quickly as I was offended, it vanished.

"You did hear what I said to you, too, right?"

I had. And it almost made it worse, which was even more stupid. The whole thing was a mess. "Just because we enjoy each other's company doesn't mean anything."

"Of course."

Trent got up from his seat, crossed the room, and leaned down over me, caging me into the chair.

I shuddered involuntarily and worked hard to control my breathing, something that was getting harder and harder to do when Trent was around.

"Brittany."

I exhaled.

"Stop overthinking this and kiss me."

I reached up and pulled his head down so I could crush his lips against mine. Instantly, heat flooded through me, and that's all it took for me to do exactly what he'd suggested. I stopped overthinking everything. The only thought on my mind involved his lips on mine. Exactly where I liked them.

Despite the alcohol that had dulled my senses not long ago, every single sense was on high alert now. That's what Trent did to me. He made me come alive.

But that's not all he did to me.

Even more startling than the things he did to my body were the things he did to my thoughts.

Trent made me think about things and even want things

that I had never in my life even considered. I wanted to tell him things. I wanted to hear his input. I enjoyed being with him. And doing things. Things that weren't only sexual.

But I liked that, too. Very much. And that's what I needed to focus on at the moment because Trent's hands were on my hips and were slipping up under my top to my breasts, and his touch on me felt amazing.

Yes.

That's what I needed to focus on.

Not on how I'd seen a different side of him at the Pines with the seniors. A softer side, a *human* side.

No. I did not need to think of that.

Nor did I need to think of how it felt when he'd crossed the room earlier at Jessie and Shane's and kissed me in front of my friends. Or the jealousy that flowed through me when he gave attention to Sandy. I didn't *get* jealous. Ever. Not about work, or my friends, and definitely not about a man.

No.

Focus, Brittany.

With a renewed effort, I concentrated on the way Trent was touching me, not that it was hard because the way he was touching me was fucking incredible. Like he knew exactly what I needed. And when I needed it.

"You need to stop thinking," Trent said as he kissed my neck in that tender spot that made me groan. "Clear your mind and don't think about anything but..." Trent slipped a hand down the front of my pants and pressed one finger to my clit. "This," he said as I groaned.

"Oh, you're good." My words were lost on my moan when he did it again. He *was* good.

"Only." He pressed again. "Think." Again. "About—Oh shit! What the—"

Trent pulled back, taking his talented fingers with him as Sheldon pounced up on the couch, directly between us.

I grabbed him up in my arms and fell back against the couch, laughing.

"What. The. Fuck..." Trent clambered backward as if Sheldon were a rabid raccoon instead of my fluffy black and white, slightly anti-social house cat. "Is that?"

I tried to stifle my laughter by burying my face in Sheldon's fur, a move he didn't take kindly to. Sheldon squirmed and mewled in protest. I held him tighter and scratched under his chin the way I knew calmed him down.

"This is Sheldon." I kissed the top of his head. "My favorite guy." He'd calmed down enough for me to let him go, and instead of jumping off the couch and running for cover under my bed, to my surprise, he padded across the cushions toward Trent, who had realized there was no significant threat from my four-legged friend and was once again sitting, albeit a little more tentatively, on the couch.

"Your cat?"

"Sheldon," I repeated. "He's been my number one for about ten years now. My longest relationship."

Trent smiled. "Is that right?"

"Oh?" I scratched Sheldon's head, making him purr and arch his back. "And you've had a longer one?"

"Would it surprise you if I had?"

"Um, yes." I laughed as Sheldon continued to walk away from me. Toward Trent.

I watched as my cat, who did not like anyone, ever—besides me—moved steadily and slowly toward Trent, who was also watching Sheldon carefully.

"Don't take it personally," I said as Sheldon stopped in front of him, assessing Trent's knee. "He doesn't like anyone. He's never actually—"

My train of thought broke off as Sheldon, without hesitation, climbed up onto Trent's lap, where he immediately settled in and started to purr.

"What were you saying about how he doesn't like anyone…"

"Traitor!"

Trent chuckled while he absentmindedly stroked Sheldon's back.

Again, a feeling I wasn't familiar with—jealousy—washed through me. I shook my head and sat back against the cushions. Getting jealous at the party earlier was one thing. But over my *cat?* That was just ridiculous.

"I see that look," Trent teased.

"What look?"

"You're jealous."

"I am not."

"You are."

His smile and the teasing tone he was using with me was making it hard to be serious. Or jealous. Which I was.

"In fact," Trent continued, "I think you're jealous that your longest relationship likes your current relationship."

"My what?"

Trent froze, but only for a second before he repeated himself. "Your relationship."

Yes. I said it. I didn't mean to say it, but I did.

And now that I had…

"Does that scare you, Brittany?"

Because shockingly, it didn't scare me the way I thought it would. Not now.

The presence of the furry, apparently anti-social cat in my lap gave me confidence that I had no right in feeling. At least not when it came to this.

"We agreed," Brittany said. "Just sex. I wouldn't really call that a—"

"Relationship?" I grinned. "That's exactly what it is, Brittany. You and me, however screwed up it is, are in a relationship."

She shook her head, looked down at her lap, and opened her mouth to object again. Before she could, I stopped her.

"Are you going to tell me about the paintings?"

Brittany's head popped up, her hair falling in a wave down her back. If the drinks she'd had earlier had clouded her in any way, she was fully alert now. "The what?"

With my free hand, I reached out and rested it on her knee. "The paintings," I said again. "The ones in the hallway, of course. But the others too. It definitely doesn't look like your interior designer put it here." They didn't. But not because they weren't worthy of hanging in Brittany's posh apartment. They were. But they had color and *life* to them. Unlike almost everything else in her place.

"Plus," I added, "I saw the easel. I didn't know you painted."

Her head spun around, her eyes landing on the easel that she clearly hadn't intended for me to see. I wished I knew why she had such high, strong walls up around her. *Who had hurt her? Why was she so hell-bent in keeping everyone out?* And the question I really wanted an answer to: *Could I be the one to break those walls down?*

Fuck. I was in trouble, and I didn't need a therapist or anyone else to tell me that. But it had finally happened. After so many years of guarding myself against this very thing, it was happening.

I was starting to care about someone other than myself.

No. Correction. I *did* care.

She still hadn't responded, so with nothing else to do, I kept talking. "You're very good." I pointed to the picture of her as a small child looking out the window. "It's incredible."

"I didn't paint that one."

A question in my eyes, I turned back to look at her. To my surprise, she wasn't trying to get up and run away. She'd settled back into the couch and although she didn't look comfortable exactly, she didn't look as if she were going to bolt. Or hit me. Both were good things.

"My father did."

Certainly, the shock was apparent on my face. "Your father?"

Brittany nodded. "He did that one before he left." She pointed to the other painting in the hall. "And that one sometime after. I never knew about it. I didn't even know my father had any idea who I was. Or where I was, but…"

I remembered what she'd said the other day. That despite not seeing her dad for a long time, he'd obviously seen her. I nodded in understanding, although there was very little I understood about the situation.

"How did you get them?"

"My mother's assistant sent them to me recently. He said he thought I should have them. My mother never even told me about them." Brittany shook her head. "She never told me that, at least in some way, my father cared enough about me to seek me out. To paint me."

I could see the tears pooling in her eyes. I squeezed her knee but gave her the space I felt she needed.

"She always told me that he chose art over us. That art was a useless pursuit that would only lead to ruin."

My gaze took in the other paintings, and the easel.

"But you paint?"

She shook her head sadly. "No. At least, I didn't. Not for a really long time. The day my mother took my paint set away, I did what I thought I was supposed to do. I focused on school. Getting good grades so I could get into a good school. That's what was important. Because with an education, I didn't have to depend on a man. I only needed myself. Art was a waste. It didn't pay the bills. It only led to heartbreak." She shook her head with a humorless chuckle. "I guess it was the same with relationships, too," she said. "My mom didn't have any friends. She never dated. Hell, she barely spoke to me. Relationships were a sign of weakness."

"She told you that?"

"She didn't have to."

Fuck. My heart ached for the little girl version of Brittany whose father had left her and a mother who didn't give her the love she deserved. The love she *needed.* Hell, my heart hurt for the adult version of Brittany, who obviously still felt the same way. Thankfully she'd seen through her mother's bullshit long enough to build the friendships she had. But even then, how close were they really? Did the girls know about the painting? Without asking, I was pretty sure I already knew the answer. There was a reason Brittany was thought of as the Ice Queen. She was protecting herself.

"Britt, I—"

"Don't feel sorry for me."

"I don't."

"You do."

She was right.

"We all have something, right? That's my *thing.*"

She tried to brush it off and make light of the sad story she'd just told me, but I wasn't laughing.

"You're right," I said slowly. "We do all have something." I took a deep breath and exhaled slowly before continuing. I didn't make it a habit to tell anyone about my own upbringing, either. Maybe we had more in common than I thought. But it felt right. "I told you I was raised by my grandparents."

She nodded, and I noticed her body soften as she recognized the turn the conversation was about to take.

"But I didn't tell you why." She shook her head and I continued. "My mom was only thirteen when she had me."

Her eyes widened in surprise. I'd expected that. "But it's not what you think," I added quickly, because the few people who had been told the story always assumed she'd been the victim of abuse. "She was in love with my dad. He was sixteen."

"Shit."

"Right?"

In my lap, Sheldon shifted and purred. The cat was oddly comforting in a way I'd never considered because I'd never actually had a pet. I scratched behind his ears until he settled again.

"They were in love," I continued. "Or as much in love as you can be at that age, when you don't know anything about anything." That got a small smile out of her. But I knew it wouldn't last. "My mother's parents blamed my father's family for the pregnancy because obviously, it had to be the boy's fault, right? They pulled her out of school and threatened to send her away to have the baby if she ever saw him again."

"Wow."

I nodded. It was all very dramatic, but it was about to get worse. This was the rough part of the story. True, I didn't actually remember any of it because I was so young when it all happened, but my grandparents had always felt it was important to know the truth. But that never seemed to make it easier. "Of course, they were young and believed they were untouchable. They didn't think my mother's parents—sorry. I can't bring myself to call them my grandparents. They don't deserve to share that title."

Brittany nodded firmly.

I knew she understood, the same way she understood that the story wouldn't have a happy ending. I continued with the story I'd only ever told a very few times. "Anyway, they couldn't comprehend that her parents could ever actually do anything to keep them apart. They were so in love, and surely their parents would see that and give them their blessing."

"I assume that didn't happen."

"Not even close." I shook my head. "My mom was about six months pregnant when they discovered them together. The way I understand it, she was really starting to show by then and people around town were starting to talk, so when they were discovered together, it was the last straw. They sent her away and despite trying everything, my father couldn't find her. When she came back, her parents had decided to raise the baby—me—as their own."

"Shit."

Again, I nodded.

"But how did you come to live with your father's parents and…"

"They killed themselves." It was a harsh way to share the truth, but also the simplest. "In true, young and stupid, Romeo-and-Juliet fashion, my parents died in a suicide pact."

Brittany's eyes widened in disbelief.

There was a reason I didn't tell people the true story. It was crazier than any fiction could possibly be. "Of course, my grandparents were devastated, and they fought for custody of me. Turns out my mother's parents were more than happy to hand me over. And that's how I came to be raised by my grandparents. They were already in their late fifties by the time they formally adopted me, and they sacrificed the rest of their lives to raise me. I'll forever be grateful for that."

"Trent." Brittany moved closer so she could put her hand on my cheek. Between us, Sheldon protested but didn't move. "I'm so sorry all of that happened to you." Her eyes shone as if she was going to cry, and despite the terrible story I'd just told, that struck me as funny.

"Are you going to cry?" I tried not to smile but failed miserably.

"No!" She pulled away and hid her face.

"You're crying."

"I am not."

"You are!" It was completely inappropriate, but I laughed anyway. "You are." I grabbed her wrists in mine and pulled her up so she was looking at me. Her cheeks were indeed damp with tears. I kissed them gently. "I didn't think you were the crying type."

"I'm not," she said. "You obviously bring it out in me."

I glanced down at the cat still happily asleep in my lap. "Sorry, buddy. Time to move." I nudged Sheldon gently until he jumped off with a mewl of protest before I pulled her in close to me.

Brittany felt good in my arms. Better than good. She felt like she belonged there. Despite the sad stories we'd just shared with each other, I didn't feel empty or lonely the way I so often did. Instead, when I laid down on the couch, pulling her up against me where I could hold her tight, I felt, for the first time, like I belonged.

Chapter Thirteen

IT HAD BEEN JUST over a week since Jessie and Shane's party where I'd drank too much, and likely made a fool of myself. It had also been just over a week since I'd fallen asleep in Trent's arms on my couch and woken up the next morning in exactly the same position.

We'd slept all night, fully clothed; his arm around me held me close, and I could honestly say I'd never had a better night's sleep in my life.

We woke to Sheldon demanding his breakfast by meowing in our faces.

Another first.

Sheldon *hated* people. Hell, he only barely tolerated me. But he'd taken to Trent immediately.

What did it mean? What did any of it mean?

Nothing.

That's what I'd told myself that morning while we drank coffee and Trent cooked a breakfast of scrambled eggs and toast in my kitchen as if it were the most natural thing in the world, instead of the scariest fucking thing ever.

Nothing. It meant nothing.

That's what I'd been telling myself all week when he texted me flirty messages or called just to say hi while he was on the East Coast, dealing with some business out there.

Nothing.

It didn't mean anything that I couldn't seem to stop myself from thinking about him and how easy it was to be with him. How natural it had felt and how he'd made me feel things I'd never felt. And I wasn't talking about sex.

Shit.

It *did* mean something.

And I wasn't sure what to do with that feeling.

But I didn't have time to dwell on it any further at the moment; I was meeting the girls for lunch and Jessie, whom I'd asked to arrive a few minutes early, had just walked through the door of the bistro.

"Hey there," she greeted me when she got to the table. "This is a nice surprise."

I stood and gave her a quick hug.

"We don't usually get to see you during the week," Jessie said. "And definitely not during the day, you workaholic." She sat across from me. "To what do we owe this pleasure, Britt? I like it."

I shook my head at her teasing, but she wasn't wrong. It had been way too long since I'd put my friends first. Hell, since I'd put *me* first.

Had I ever?

"I like it, too." I smiled at my friend, focusing only on her. "And I'm so glad you could meet me a little early. I actually wanted to apologize for the other night at your house. I shouldn't have had so many drinks and—"

"Yeah, that was interesting."

Leave it to Jessie to tell me how she really feels.

"But you don't need to apologize for it," she added. "I just thought it was unusual because you don't usually drink, let alone to the point where you need to be taken home."

"Technically, I didn't need to be taken home. I just…"

There was nothing I could say, so I simply shrugged instead. "Anyway, I'm sorry. I'm not sure what happened."

"Is it Trent?"

I sat back in my seat. "Trent? Why would it be—"

"Are you really going to sit across from me and try to tell me that you're not completely into him? Really?" She tipped her head in challenge.

And of course I was up for that particular challenge.

"I'm not into Trent."

"Liar." Jessie said the word with a grin as the waitress arrived. She ordered a glass of white wine; I stuck with my soda water. "You're totally into him," she said when the waitress retreated. "Anyone can see it."

"No, they can't."

They couldn't, could they?

"And I'm not—"

"He's totally into you, too."

"What?"

"Oh…yes." She wiggled her eyebrows. "I have to admit, Britt. I wasn't sure I'd ever see the day that your feelings for a man got you so worked up."

"It's not that I was…" I let my objection trail off because what was the point? She wasn't wrong. And there didn't seem to be a reason to fight it any longer. "Okay," I admitted. "I was worked up." It felt good to say it out loud. "Trent gets me worked up."

Jessie's eyes flashed, and I didn't miss it.

"Okay," I continued. "I admit it. He gets under my skin."

"Under your skin?"

I nodded. "It's more than that." I might as well just come all the way clean at this point. "He makes me feel things."

"Oh ya?" Jessie didn't try to hide her surprise. "He makes you feel things?"

"A lot of things."

"Tell me."

I shook my head. It was one thing to tell my friend a few details, but it was a completely different thing to tell her *all* of the details, especially the ones I wasn't ready to admit to myself yet.

"What kind of things, Britt?" Jessie's voice was low, searching.

I squeezed my eyes.

But why?

Why shouldn't I tell her exactly how I felt about Trent? About how he made me feel things I'd never felt before. How he made me *think* things I'd never thought of before. How he'd made me...hell. How he'd made me believe that I could be something I'd never been.

How could one man do all of that?

Without even trying.

Damn.

"It's okay, Britt," Jessie said. "You're allowed to talk about it, you know? Nothing bad will happen if you say what you're thinking." She ducked her head with a small smile. "Or even, what you're feeling."

I shook my head. "Oh, shit, Jessie. You don't even know what you're saying."

"I do."

"No," I said. "You don't."

I didn't even know what she was saying. But I was pretty sure I had an idea. Trent challenged me. He made me think of a future I'd never considered. He made me feel...loved.

Had I ever felt loved before? Really *loved?*

I wasn't sure I had. Not the way Trent *loved me.*

Love.

No. I couldn't let myself think that way. Not even for a moment.

"Hey." Jessie's hand grabbed mine across the table. "Talk to me, Britt."

"I don't know what you're talking about."

"You do." She squeezed my hand and looked me sharply in the eye. "Stop denying it. You know exactly what I'm talking about. And it's okay. I promise."

I'd been on the East Coast for just over a week, and I was dying to get home.

Home.

That's what Aspen Valley was now.

Home.

Because that's where Brittany was.

And despite every single thing I'd ever thought about how my life would go, both my mind *and* my heart were telling me unequivocally that Aspen Valley was home.

Brittany.

No. The only thing my heart, and particularly my body, was telling me, was…*Brittany.*

And being away from her for a whole week was *way* too long.

I moved through the MultiTech office front door quickly and as if there were a line pulling me, I moved straight across the lobby, past where we'd crashed together on the floor, the first time our eyes locked and it led to a private moment in her office that led to…

Well. *Fuck.*

I needed to get to my woman.

My. Woman.

I didn't even try to deny it to myself or anyone else who

bothered to ask me. Brittany was my woman. I'd fight anyone who challenged me on that. Not that they would, because…*Brittany*.

I knocked sharply on her office door.

Nothing.

I knocked again. Twice. Harder.

Still nothing.

I leaned in, trying to hear what might be happening on the other side of her office door. I knocked again. "Britt?"

Fuck this.

I turned her handle and opened the door to an empty office.

It was eleven thirty on a Wednesday. Where else would she be? Brittany was *always* in the office.

"She's not here."

I spun around to see Shane, watching me with a wry smile on his face.

"Where is she?"

He shrugged. "Let's go for lunch." He nodded toward the door. "Unless you have other plans."

I didn't. Not if Brittany wasn't there. Because my plans *had* been to bend her over her desk. *Yes.* A week had been *way* too long to be away from her. Way too long to feel her curves pressed up against me, her soft skin under my rough hands as I explored all parts of her. Far too many days had passed since I felt her body tighten around me as I pushed her over the edge into climax after climax.

But as much as I'd missed all of that, it wasn't the only thing I missed. Besides a few texts and one, very short phone call, I hadn't spoken to Brittany the entire time I'd been gone. And to my surprise, that had been the hardest part. In a very short time, I'd grown very used to talking to her about silly little things, and the big ones, too. I craved seeing her sexy smile light up her beautiful face.

Lunch with Shane would be a lackluster consolation prize. But at least it was something.

"Sure." I turned away from her office door. "Why not?"

We went to the Aspen Valley Country Club, where we ordered steak sandwiches and made small talk about the office until our food was delivered.

"Looks like my office space will be secured next week," I told Shane. "So I'll finally be getting out of your way. I can't thank you enough for lending me the room while I was sorting things out."

He waved off my thanks. "So I take it you'll be staying in Aspen Valley then? Things are going well here for you."

I could tell by the tone of his voice that he was referring to a lot more than just business, but I wasn't going to bite. Whatever was going on with Brittany and me could stay between us. At least until I knew exactly what was going on.

"It is," I said. "This town is booming and absolutely ripe with opportunity. It would be foolish for me *not* to have an office here. My staff will come in next week to get things set up and—"

"You know that's not what I meant."

I shrugged and cut into my steak. "I'm not talking about it."

"I heard a rumor," Shane continued, as if he hadn't heard me.

"About my new office?"

"About a certain blonde we both know."

"I told you, I'm not talking about it." I popped the steak in my mouth and chewed slowly.

"Talking about what? How these women have a way of getting under our skin in a way that we just can't shake?"

I stared at my old friend. There was no way he could know how I was feeling about Brittany. Was there?

"Sounds like I showed up at the right time?" Phillip

Conrad appeared next to our table. "Mind if I join you guys? I was going to grab a bite on my own, but…"

"Of course." Shane waved to an empty chair.

"Are we talking about the women?" Phillip said as soon as he was settled.

Shane laughed. "You know it."

I took another bite of my lunch, not willing to participate in this discussion. Phillip and Shane had totally different situations than I did. They just didn't know it. Brittany and I had agreed. Just sex. And even if I might be changing my mind on that, it didn't change the fact that that's exactly what we had. An agreement.

The tender, perfectly cooked steak suddenly tasted like dirt in my mouth. I reached for my water glass and swallowed hard.

Hell, I couldn't even convince myself that Brittany didn't mean anything to me.

"Not going to lie, buddy," Shane said to me. "I didn't think I'd ever see the day Brittany would settle down."

I almost choked on my food. "Settle down?" I said when I'd recovered. "No one is talking about settling down. That's not what this is."

It was sex.

That's what it was. It wasn't settling down. Not. Even. Close.

"I don't know what happened to the two of you," I said, abandoning my lunch altogether. "But that's not what's happening with Britt. We're just enjoying each other's company."

"Oh, yes." Phillip smiled. "I think we've both heard all about how much you're enjoying each other's company."

I knew Brittany was talking about our sexual exploits with her girlfriends; after all, that had been the entire purpose of our agreement. But I didn't make it a habit to kiss and tell. A fact I relayed to the guys.

"Look," I said after a moment. "I know the stories." I turned to Phillip. "You were always in love with Abby. Now you're together." He nodded, and I turned to Shane. "You and Jessie started out as just sex. But now you're inseparable." He nodded as well. "Brittany and me...it's different with us."

There was no way I was going to tell either of them that I'd wanted the woman from the moment I'd laid eyes on her and now that I had her, I didn't want to let her go with a ferocity that was beginning to consume me.

No, I couldn't tell them that, because that's not how this was going to play out.

She wanted temporary.

She didn't *do* relationships.

Neither did I.

But...it was getting harder and harder to remember that. Especially when the only thing I could think about was how she felt in my arms. How she made soft, little, vulnerable squeaks in her sleep. And especially how I'd never shared such intimate details about my childhood with another woman before. And how it had only felt natural to tell Brittany those things and for her to tell me her secrets, too. How despite not having sex with her that night, it had been the single most intimate night of my life. And waking up with her still in my arms the next morning had been the best morning of my entire life.

Yes. Remembering that my relationship with Brittany wasn't real was becoming almost impossible.

Especially because I was pretty sure I'd changed my mind.

"I'm sure it is different," Phillip said.

I pulled myself from my thoughts back to my friends, who were watching me strangely.

"But it's the same, too."

"As much as I appreciate your input, guys, I'll tell you

what." I tossed my napkin to the table and stood to leave. "How about when I want your opinions, I'll ask for it. Now if you'll excuse me, there's something I need to do."

Too much time had already gone by without seeing her. Instead of talking *about* Brittany, I wanted to talk *to* her.

"She won't be back at the office," Shane said, stopping me in my tracks.

I turned slowly and looked at him in question.

"She's taken a leave."

"A leave?" My gut churned.

"A leave of absence," Shane said. For the first time, his face was serious as he said, "I'm sorry, Trent. I honestly thought you knew."

After having lunch with the girls, I knew what I needed to do. I also knew it had to be done immediately before I could change my mind. I called Shane and told him I would be taking a leave of absence. I assured him I'd be available for questions via email and phone calls, but no, I did not have time to train anyone or wait a few days before leaving. The leave would be effective immediately.

What I needed to do had to be done right away.

He agreed, reluctantly, the way I knew he would. I'd worked hard for Shane; he knew more than almost anyone how much I deserved a break.

As soon as we disconnected the call, I called Fraser, my mother's old assistant. Just as I'd predicted, he had the information I desired. In fact, it was almost as if he knew I'd be calling and was ready with it. I didn't have time to dig into that. I had more important things to do.

The next call I made was to my assistant, Julie.

"I need you to book me a flight to Vancouver," I said

without preamble. "As soon as you can. One way. And schedule the cat sitter."

Of course, she had questions, but like the good assistant she was, she got the job done efficiently and quickly. Twenty minutes later, I was home. Sheldon sat on my bed, watching me suspiciously as I pulled my suitcase out of the closet and started to pack. "I'm sorry, buddy," I said to the cat. "I know you don't like it when I leave, but the nice cat sitter will feed you and make sure your box is clean. She might even pet you if you let her and don't hide under my bed the entire time I'm gone."

Sheldon growled, but it turned to a purr as soon as I scratched his head.

I probably could have asked Trent to look in on him. After all, Trent was the only other human Sheldon tolerated, and maybe even liked a little. But that would mean I'd have to call Trent. And I couldn't do that yet.

Not until I had answers.

I didn't even know the questions yet, but I would. And when I had answers to those questions, then, if it wasn't too late, I'd talk to Trent. And I couldn't even begin to guess how that conversation would go.

The only thing I knew for sure was that I was forty-one years old and for almost my entire life, I'd lived by a set of rules that no longer made sense—if they ever had—and it was long past time for a change.

And the only way I knew to initiate that change was to find him.

My father.

Chapter Fourteen

SHE WAS GONE.

I'd been to her apartment, where the doorman told me so. He wasn't at liberty to tell me where or for how long, no matter how much money I slipped him. However, for a hundred-dollar bill, he did assure me that Sheldon was cared for.

It was a small relief, but one all the same.

My calls went to voicemail. My text messages went unread.

Shane claimed he didn't know where she was going, and when two days later, I finally tracked down her assistant, Julie, I was told, quite definitively, that she was under very clear directions not to tell anyone of Brittany's whereabouts for any reason whatsoever and that the next time she spoke with her boss, she'd let Brittany know I'd inquired about her.

Fuck.

It wasn't enough. I needed more. I needed to talk to her, see her...just...*fuck.*

With nowhere else to go, I went to the only place I could think of.

The mountains.

The proximity of the mountains was one of the best things about Aspen Valley. Besides, of course, Brittany.

Brittany.

I pressed my foot down on the accelerator, pushing my car as far as I could. Anything to get me there faster and away from this town where Brittany was supposed to be.

Brittany.

The moment I left the city behind, I unrolled my windows and let the piney freshness wash through me. It helped. I could feel my blood pressure lowering. But it wasn't enough. I whipped my car into the parking space and quickly changed into the shorts, T-shirt, and sneakers I left in my gym bag in the trunk before taking off at a sprint up the trail.

It had been a long time but my body remembered what to do. I pushed myself along the windy mountain trail, ducking low-hanging branches, jumping over roots and rocks that littered the path, digging deep with the steep elevation until finally, my lungs burned, my muscles strained, and mercifully, my mind cleared.

The thing about pushing your body almost to its physical breaking point was that there wasn't room for any other thoughts beyond survival.

Which was why trail running had been my salvation for all the hardest points of my life. Especially when my grandparents passed away and I found myself truly alone for the first time. I'd run in the mountains until my body shook from the exertion. I'd sit on a rocky outcropping and look out at the world below while I caught my breath and my heart rate returned to normal. And I'd talk to my grandma and grandpa. It was the only place I felt close to them. Like they could hear me.

With a final push, I broke through the forested trail, and out into the sunlight at the top of the mountain I'd chosen. I dropped my head and almost folded in half as I worked to catch my breath before sitting down.

It wasn't until my heart rate had slowed and the sweat had started to dry on my skin that I spoke. "I think I'm in love with her." Saying the words out loud didn't feel scary or strange. They felt right, but not completely. There was a whisper of wind and despite the warm day, the hairs on my arms stood up. I dropped my gaze for a moment. "No," I corrected myself when I looked up. "I don't have to think about it. I *am* in love with her. I've never felt this way about a woman before. She challenges me and pushes me and at the same time, she's soft and caring in the most unexpected way. I can talk to her unlike anyone ever before." I swallowed hard. "Except for you guys."

I never had a typical grandparent/grandchild relationship with them. It wasn't a parent/child relationship either. It was a special combination of all of it, plus more. Grandpa and I would spend time camping and fishing in the woods, where we'd talk about all kinds of things. Important things. About life. And with Grandma, we'd hike and explore. She'd show me the native plants and mushrooms and she'd *listen*. She always knew the right thing to say and when to say it.

When they died, I'd lost so much more than my grandparents who were like parents to me. I'd lost my ability to open up and be listened to.

Until Brittany.

"I'm not sure she loves me," I told them. "It hasn't been very long. But you always told me there wasn't a timeline on love or relationships, and I see that now. I thought maybe she might...but...now she's gone. Not forever," I added quickly. "At least I don't think so. But that's the whole problem. I don't *know* anything. She didn't tell me where she was going, or when she'd be back and..."

I let my thoughts trail away, suddenly missing their words of wisdom more than ever. I let the sounds of the mountains fill me instead. The cry of an eagle soared next to the cliff, catching the thermals to lift higher into the air. The gentle chirping of the unseen crickets on the hillside behind me. The occasional rustle of the wind in the trees when it gusted. But otherwise, it was silent.

It wasn't like me to be so affected by…well, anyone. And that's how I knew.

Brittany wasn't just anyone.

And I was going to make sure she knew it.

By the time I made my way, slower this time, down the mountain, I knew exactly what I needed to do. But first, I had one more stop to make.

Thanks to Fraser, who'd sent me the information I'd asked for, along with a request to call him when I landed, I knew exactly where I was going, and I didn't waste any time. I gave the cab driver the address and settled in, staring out the window, not really seeing anything at all.

After a few minutes, I pulled my cell phone from my purse and powered it on. I'd silenced all incoming calls and messages, but I wasn't surprised to see that dozens more had come in while I'd been in the air. I knew I'd ignore all of them.

For now.

My eye caught on Trent's name halfway down the screen. He'd called and messaged a few times. My breath caught in my throat, as I pressed the screen to reveal his messages.

Hey baby. I'm back. When can I see your sexy ass?

Britt? You weren't at the office. I had some dirty plans for that desk. Let me know when you'll be in.

Brittany. Call me.

. . .

I'm worried, Brittany. Let me know you're okay. Please.

Hot tears pricked at my eyes, but there was no way I was going to cry because a man I was only supposed to be having casual sex with told me he was worried about me. *Pull it together, Brittany.*

I could chastise myself all I wanted, but I knew exactly where the tears had come from, and why. Trent was the entire reason I'd dropped everything and gotten on a plane.

I started to type in a response, to tell him I was fine and I'd call him in a few days, but changed my mind.

I needed to do this on my own. I needed to do it for myself.

That was important.

Once more, I powered my phone off and tucked it away so I could stare out the window.

"We're here." The voice jerked me awake. "Ma'am? We're here."

I must have drifted off. I swiped at my face, made my apologies to the driver, and paid the man before gathering my things.

I had no reason to doubt that the information Fraser had given me wasn't accurate, but I was surprised when I looked up to see that I was not standing in front of an apartment building, or a house, or…anything, but a large mural painted on the side of a building.

I turned around to grab the cab again before he took off, but it was too late. He was gone.

With few options, I pulled my carry-on suitcase behind me and walked toward the mural that looked vaguely familiar.

It was bright but had the feeling of being subdued at the same time, as if the artist had held back. It was a painting of a family, but they didn't look happy. They all stood slightly apart from each other, as if there were something keeping them apart.

A tear slipped down my throat when I recognized myself in the center of the mural. My mother to the side, her mouth set in a hard line. But her eyes told a different story. One of regret. It was my father I focused on the longest. It had been a long time since I'd seen him, but he looked exactly as I remembered. He stood to the other side of me, his arm outstretched as if he were trying but couldn't reach me. His eyes were full of pain, but despite reaching for me, they were focused directly on my mother.

The entire image was haunting, yet beautiful.

"It's called *Regret.*"

I spun at the voice.

Fraser Lawrence, my mother's assistant, stood a few feet away, watching me.

"Fraser? What are you doing here?"

"I asked you to call me when you landed."

"But…" Of course, I hadn't called. I'd no intention to. "But why are you here?"

His lips flicked up in a grin. "Because I knew you wouldn't." He strode across the concrete and held his arms out for a hug.

I'd known the man almost my whole life. Every birthday card, or Christmas present, was sent from him. I'd always known it was Fraser who reminded her to call me on special occasions, and I'd grown to care about him almost as a replacement parent. After all, he'd cared more than the other two combined.

"In some ways, you are very much like your mother, Brittany," he said when he stepped back. "That's how I knew you wouldn't call. But in most other ways, you are very different. Which is how I knew you'd need me here to explain all this."

I inhaled deeply and looked up at the mural again. "I don't understand," I said after a moment. "I thought you were giving me my father's address?"

"I did."

The nod of his head told me what I'd long suspected.

"He passed away shortly after painting this," he continued. "Fifteen years ago."

Despite the fact that in my heart, I'd felt my father was gone, I still felt the sharp sting of loss.

"I'm sorry," Fraser continued. "I wanted her to tell you. I wanted her to tell you everything. And now that she's gone, well, I no longer feel the same sense of loyalty. I should have done this years ago." The older man gestured to a bench in a grassy park area across the street from the mural.

"Your mother was a very smart woman," he said once we were seated with a better view of the painting. "Very driven and as you know, very successful."

I nodded.

"But she was a terrible mother."

I couldn't help it; I burst out in one quick, sharp laugh.

"I saw it," Fraser continued. "So did she." His gaze softened. "She loved you very much, but she was terrible at showing you that love or giving it to you."

I didn't bother saying anything, because there was nothing to do but agree.

"Your dad didn't leave when you were ten. She sent him away."

"What?" I shook my head. "No. He left. She said—"

"She said a lot of things."

Fraser put his hand over my hand. The touch was unexpectedly settling.

"I know this is hard to understand, but she loved your father very much, despite everything. When they met, he was so sure he would be a famous artist one day, and because he was so sure, she believed it, too. But passion and talent didn't pay the bills and as time went on, Patrick wasn't selling enough art; he wasn't hitting it big the way he'd been so sure he would. Your mother wanted him to go back to school, get a real job, or even teach painting lessons. But he wouldn't. Finally, it was too much for her. She hit her breaking point. She confided in me that she saw you had some of the same artistic tendencies, and she was terrified you'd grow up and choose the starving artist lifestyle instead of being happy. Or what she thought would make you happy. So she sent him away."

It didn't make sense. "She *sent* him away? But I needed a father. I needed—"

"She was sure you needed stability. A future. So that's what she gave you." Fraser looked tired. As if keeping the secret all this time had exhausted him. "Your father agreed because he loved you. And he loved her, too. He would have done anything for the two of you. But he never stopped loving you." Fraser pointed toward the mural again. "I think that's clear."

I sat in silence for a few minutes, letting it all soak in. It was a terrible story, but I believed it. It sounded exactly like something my mother would do. And Fraser had no reason to lie. Especially now that she was gone.

"I wish I could have told you earlier, Brittany. But...I..."

"You were sworn to secrecy," I finished for him. I'm sure it was more complicated than that, with a nondisclosure agreement—never mind the fact that I was always convinced that Fraser was secretly in love with my mother. "It's okay. It's not your fault."

"I know it's not much," he said. "But your mother had this park put in as a memorial to your father. I truly believe she never quit loving him either." I saw the flash of pain in Fraser's eyes when he spoke. "I didn't agree with her methods," he said. "But I do think she wanted the best for you."

I didn't disagree with that. Not really. She wasn't the

mother I wanted nor the one I needed. But she was the one I'd had. "Why send me the paintings, Fraser? Why now?"

He turned to me and took my hands in his. "I see you, Brittany. As I said, you are so much like her. But so different, too. You have a lot of your father in you, too. They both made mistakes in raising you and keeping you from him. And keeping themselves from each other. They denied not only you the love you needed, but themselves as well." He shook his head, lost in a memory for a moment. "I'll never truly understand why they made the choices they did. But it wasn't your fault. It never was. You deserved more. You still do." He looked me in the eyes then. "Don't let their mistakes become yours, too. Life is too short not to have it all. Success and love—you can have both. Your mother never understood that, but it's my hope that you will." He squeezed my hands tight in his. "Don't let life pass you by without allowing yourself that."

Success and *love*.

You can have both.

"Where's that pretty little girlfriend of yours today, Trent?" Flo turned her head to accept my kiss on her cheek.

"Maybe she decided she likes them a little older," Roy said with a wiggle of his bushy eyebrows that earned him a light smack on the arm from his wife. "I didn't mean me, obviously," he said with a wink as I sat down.

"That's actually why I'm here today," I said without preamble. "I mean, you know I love visiting you both, but—"

"There's no Bingo today," Roy said with a matter-of-fact nod.

"Oh, Trent. You know we love seeing you no matter when you can get here."

Florence's warmth calmed me a little. The run had helped

a lot. But I'd underestimated how powerful kind words could be. I felt better immediately, and I hadn't even told them anything about Brittany.

Flo reached for my hand. "Ignore him," she said with a smile. "He's an old man. Now, tell us why you're here today. Is Brittany okay?"

I nodded. "She's fine. Actually," I corrected myself quickly. "I think she's fine. I mean, she *should* be fine. I'm just—"

"Take a breath, dear." Flo squeezed my hand. "Tell us what's going on between the two of you. Are you having a disagreement? It happens sometimes and it's perfectly normal."

"Lord knows, we've had our fair share of disagreements," Roy chimed in with a grin. "Piece of advice—all you have to do is tell her you're wrong and she's right." He grinned. "It works every time."

"I don't doubt it does." I chuckled. "But I'm afraid this might be more serious than that."

The old man's brows knitted together, and Florence made a noise somewhere between a sigh and a gasp. Instantly, I was certain I was blowing it all out of proportion. I shook my head and tried again. "No, it's not…it's just…I think I'm in love with her."

Neither of them reacted right away. Instead, they stared blankly at me, then looked at each other. And that's when they erupted in laughter, as if they'd coordinated it.

Taken off guard, I sat back in my chair. I wasn't used to having people laugh at me. Ever. Especially when I'd just confided my deepest secret.

What the actual—

Flo was the first to recover from her laughing fit. "Oh, Trent." She shook her head slowly. "Of course you love her."

"No." I squeezed the bridge of my nose. "You don't under-stand. I wasn't…we weren't… we—"

"It was clear to everyone how much the two of you care for each other," Roy said. "You two were the talk of the dining room that night."

"We were what?"

"It's true," Florence confirmed. "Don't underestimate how happy it makes us oldies to see young love."

We were hardly young, but I didn't see the point in arguing that particular detail with them.

"But we're getting off track," Flo said. "I don't see what the problem is when it comes to love."

Her husband made a noise he tried to cover with a cough. "Flo, darling," he said, a thread of laughter in his voice. "Loving a woman is almost always the problem."

"Roy. This is serious."

She chastised him, but I didn't miss the smile on her face. Their easy banter and obvious affection they had for each other was the entire reason I was here trying to ask for advice. But it was starting to feel like I might not get what I was seeking.

"Trent." Flo grabbed my attention again. "Talk, sweetheart. What's going on with Brittany?"

They were both watching me intently now, so I took a breath and told them the truth. We weren't really dating. She was doing me a favor. I subtly left out the part about how we were having hot sex partly so she could tell her friends all about it. There were certain lines I wasn't willing to cross and telling a sweet senior citizen couple about our exploits was definitely one of those lines.

"But now," I continued with my story, "it's turned into more than pretending."

Flo nodded knowingly.

I gave her a questioning look.

"It always does," she said confidently. "And if the two of you were pretending the other day…well, let's just say…"

"Neither of you had to work very hard," her husband finished for her.

"Are you saying…"

They nodded together. "We said it before. It was pretty obvious that the two of you have feelings for each other."

They *had* said that before, and I wanted to believe it. I did. I really did. Because literally, every moment that passed helped concrete it for me. I was forty-two, and I could confidently say I'd never one time felt the way I was feeling right now. A twisted, turned inside-out feeling where my entire body yearned for her. For the sound of her voice, the touch of her hand on mine. Her smile, her presence.

I couldn't stop thinking about her. Every single thought was completely consumed by her. My own thoughts and feelings were starting to be tangled up with hers. I cared, I worried, I wondered…hell, I was bordering on obsessed.

Despite the fact that this was a completely brand-new feeling to me, I knew Roy and Flo were right: I was madly and deeply in love with Brittany Donahue. It had happened both suddenly and gradually. But no matter how it had happened, it had. And now, there was no going back. At least not for me.

But…

It wasn't just me.

I dropped my head and shook it a little before looking up again. "It's not just me, though. And even if you're right and she feels the same way about me"—*fuck, I hoped she did*—"I don't know where she is right now. She left, and didn't tell me and…well, she's…"

"She's a scared little kitten."

Florence spoke with so much conviction that anything I was going to say vanished from my brain. I stared at the older woman, but she merely nodded and crossed her arms over her chest.

"Once upon a time, Roy and I had a ranch house. Just a

small property with a few cattle, nothing like the operations today."

I looked to Roy, who nodded his confirmation.

"And we'd always have barn cats. An almost constant stream of them. Mostly they were pretty feral. They lived outside and took care of the mice."

"But every once in a while, a coyote would leave a litter of kittens orphaned." Roy took over the story. "I'd bring them in to Flo, and she'd nestle them into an old towel-lined box and feed them goat's milk from an eyedropper."

Flo smiled with the memory. "And they were all the same, Trent." She looked at me knowingly. "They'd scratch and hiss and panic when you got close. Their instinct was to run away and hide. So do you know what I'd do?"

It was a rhetorical question, so I waited.

"I'd love them," she said after a moment. "I'd hold them close, pet them, and love them. And after a while, they started to realize that not only was I not going to hurt them, I was going to keep on loving them. I would be there for them, take care of them when they needed it and always...love them."

"So you're saying..."

"Brittany's a scared little kitten."

Next to her, Roy nodded in agreement. "Just love her, Trent. She'll stop hissing and scratching eventually." He chuckled and Flo smacked his arm lightly. Undeterred, he added, "It might not hurt if you gave her a little pet, too."

He blew a kiss at his wife, and that time, all three of us laughed.

Chapter Fifteen

FRASER SAT with me for over an hour. He answered all of my questions. And more that I didn't even know I had.

It was hard to reconcile the fact that my mother had been directly responsible for sending my father away. And even more difficult to believe that he could leave me. There was a lot to digest and process, but it felt better than I expected it would to finally know the truth. A peace settled over me when I finally got off the park bench and made my way back to the hotel I'd booked for the night.

Once I'd checked in, I took a long bubble bath, something that for the life of me I couldn't remember ever doing. I closed my eyes and let my thoughts drift through everything that had happened over the last few weeks.

Trent. My mother. The paintings. Trent. My father. My own painting. Trent.

I felt bad that I hadn't returned his calls or texts. Or told him I was leaving, or...well, I felt bad about it all. He didn't deserve to be ghosted. Not that I was ghosting him. I wasn't. But I didn't know what to say. Or how to say it. And maybe leaving without a word was the chicken way out of...well, whatever it was that was happening between us, but it was the only way I knew how to deal with my feelings.

At the time.

Know better, do better.

Isn't that how the saying went?

And now I knew...

Well, I sure as hell didn't know *better*. But I knew *more*. And maybe that would have to be good enough.

I pulled myself from the now lukewarm water and wrapped myself in the fluffy white robe that hung on the wall. I felt better than I had in a very long time, as if the water that slowly spiraled down the drain took with it all my problems and stresses, leaving me cleansed of my past.

I almost laughed aloud at myself.

One bubble bath, and here I was turning into a completely different person. Darla would be very impressed with me that her *woo-woo* ways were finally rubbing off on me, even in the slightest way.

I settled myself into the fluffy bed and pulled out my phone.

I was done hiding.

From everything.

I pressed the buttons and a moment later, just the face I needed to see lit up the screen.

"Britt!" Jessie practically yelled into her phone. "Where the hell have you been? Everyone is worried sick. I even tried bribing Julie with...well, never mind. She's unmovable, that assistant of yours. Seriously. She wouldn't budge. Anyway... hold on. Let me get the other girls in here."

"Wait, Jessie, I—"

Too late. A moment later, Sandy and Abby's faces popped up on the screen as well. I was hoping to talk to each of them individually, but then again...when had we ever done anything separately?

"Where's Darla?"

"Here I am."

With all four of them staring back at me from my phone screen, I suddenly felt better about everything that had happened in the last twenty-four hours.

It's true that you can't choose your family, but you *can* choose your friends who become family. It was long past time I let my *true family* in.

"Okay," Jessie said. "What's going on, Brittany? Are you okay?"

Tears burned my eyes when I nodded. "I am. At least, I am now. And I think I'll be a lot better soon." I took a deep breath. "There's a lot I'd like to tell you, girls, if that's okay with you?"

Sandy smiled. "You know it is, Britt."

"It's always been okay," Jessie said.

"We were waiting for you to be ready." Abby nodded.

"Ready?"

"We know you better than anyone, Brittany." It was Darla who answered. "And we've always known that there's more to your workaholic tendencies than just the drive to succeed. But we didn't want to push you because you needed to work it out for yourself."

Confused, I looked at my friends' faces in turn. "You mean, you've known all this time that my mother sent my father away and he died fifteen years ago?"

"Whoa." Jessie held up a hand. "We did not know that."

"No," Abby said. "Shit, Brittany. I'm so sorry. We didn't know that."

"Then what *did* you know?"

Darla laughed softly. "Silly girl. We knew you were hurting and you didn't even know it. We could all see it, even if you couldn't."

"And it was our job as your best friends just to love you," Sandy said. "So that's what we did."

They'd definitely done that. And they'd done a damn good job of it, too.

The tears that had been threatening spilled down my cheeks in streams. For the first time in recent memory, I didn't try to stop them or stifle them. I just let them come while I told them the whole story about my mother, my father, and how Fraser had filled in all the blanks for me. I told them everything, including the way I used to love to paint until my mom had taken my supplies away and shamed me for being like my father. I told them how I'd felt compelled to pick up the brush again, and how I'd been experimenting with paint once more. I saw the look of surprise on their faces with that acknowledgment. But no judgment. Not once.

They accepted my story and like the true friends they were, they all cried a little with me.

When I was finished, Sandy pressed her phone up against her chest. "That's me hugging you," she said when her face filled the screen again. "I wish I could give you a hug in person, Britt."

"Me too," Abby said. "Shit. That's a lot, Brittany."

"I'm sorry you didn't feel you could talk about it with us before." Jessie pressed her lips together. "But I'm glad you're talking now."

"It's not you," I said quickly, lest they feel it was something they'd done that had kept me quiet. "I didn't talk about it at all. I don't think I even let myself think about it very much," I admitted. "I finally hit a point where I realized my mom was never going to be the mom I wanted, and my dad was gone, so I just kind of compartmentalized it all and threw myself into work."

"It makes sense," Darla said. "And for whatever it's worth, your energy feels totally different now, even through the phone."

"My energy?" I tried not to laugh at Darla's hippie tendencies, especially because I agreed with her. I felt different, too.

"What about Trent?" It was Abby who asked. "What does he think about everything? Have you talked to him?"

"He's been looking for you," Jessie said.

"I know." I nodded. "And the answer is…yes and no. I mean, I actually told him some things the other day. More than I've ever told anyone before…" I let the thought drift away. "But no. I didn't tell him I was leaving town, and I haven't spoken to him yet, and…"

"Why not?" Sandy asked.

"It doesn't….we're not…" I took a breath and looked down. "I'm scared," I answered truthfully. I'd had enough of hiding things from my friends. Or myself. "I'm scared of how I feel about him." Saying the words out loud wasn't as terrifying as I thought, and when I looked up again, I was staring into four smiling faces. "What?"

"You like him," Abby said.

"We *knew* that!" Jessie laughed.

"But she *really* likes him," Sandy added. "Maybe *like* like."

I groaned. "It's not like that," I admitted. "It was just sex. We were *going for it*. You know, same as Jessie and Abby did. I even told him about the pact, and he was totally good about it." *Better than good*, I thought, but didn't say as the image of some of our sexiest times flashed through my memory. "But it was just sex," I said again. "That's it."

I was absolutely certain that all four of them would issue objections immediately. But to my surprise, all four of them were silent.

Abby raised her eyebrows. Sandy tried not to smile, and Darla stifled a giggle, but it was Jessie who finally said, "You said it yourself. It *was* just sex." She paused. "But what is it *now?*"

Some might say what I did after leaving the Pines and getting clarity from Flo and Roy was crossing the line. And yes, others might say it was breaking and entering. But I didn't care. There was only one thing I cared about when I bribed the cat sitter I spotted coming out of Brittany's building with a thousand dollars, along with character references, and a small lie that Brittany wanted me to take care of Sheldon because the cat so obviously liked me, and no, she shouldn't bother calling Ms. Donahue; she was very busy.

It wasn't until I convinced the woman, who rather obviously was dressed in a sweatshirt with a cat head on it, to take me up to the condo so she could see for herself that Sheldon—who didn't like anyone—really did like me.

Sure enough, Sheldon ran right to me, and the cat lady—convinced that I was legit and that most importantly, Sheldon would be well cared for—left me alone in Brittany's apartment.

We were going to have to have a conversation about the security of a woman who carried a cat-shaped bag, but first things first.

Brittany.

I still had no idea where she'd gone or when she'd be back, but I didn't care. I'd made my decision, and I'd wait as long as it took. I was fully prepared to order food and supplies for the next few months if that's what I needed to do.

As it turned out, I only had to wait overnight. I was making coffee in Brittany's white kitchen the next morning, Sheldon on the counter next to me eating from a can of tuna I'd found in the cupboard, when I heard the key in the door.

I froze. Sheldon's ears pricked up.

Neither of us moved.

"Sheldon?" Brittany's voice rang out. "Mommy's home."

Mommy?

It was cute. Unexpected, but very cute.

The cat looked toward the hallway and Brittany's voice, up at me, and finally back to the can of tuna.

"Sheldon?" Her voice was flecked with concern, but it died on her lips when she walked around the corner. "Where are—"

"Hi." I raised my hand in a wave and looked down at the cat, who was licking the now empty can. I shrugged. "Sorry."

"What are you doing here?" Brittany moved closer.

She was dressed in what I was quickly coming to think of as her *casual* look. Black pants, a silky blouse, and a jacket. I wasn't entirely sure she even owned jeans. Still, she looked gorgeous with her long blonde hair hanging down her back. My eyes locked in on her red lips. It had been far too long since I'd kissed them. Despite her polished appearance, Brittany looked tired, like maybe she'd been crying.

"And," she continued as she took another step closer, "why is Sheldon on the counter?"

The cat looked up and meowed.

"And why is he eating tuna?"

"I thought it was what he ate," I said lamely. "I didn't realize he wasn't allowed on the counter." I looked down as the cat looked up at me. "You played me," I said to him.

Sheldon meowed again as Brittany picked him up.

I was certain she was going to be pissed, but to my surprise, there was a small smile on her face. "You still didn't answer my question."

"I told you." I held up my hands in surrender. "The cat played me. He really is a devious little shit."

She laughed openly then. "No." Her voice was muffled when she nuzzled her face into the cat's fur before setting him down. On the floor. "Why are you here, Trent?"

Brittany stood in front of me, the question hanging between us. There were a million ways I could answer it, but only one I wanted to use. I took a breath and looked her straight in the eyes. "Because I'm in love with you."

The words slipped from my tongue easily. As if I was always meant to say them.

She didn't react, so I said it again. This time as I took a step closer to her and reached for her hand. "I'm in love with you, Brittany." I spoke each word clearly, so there was no mistaking them. "I'm not sure when it happened, or how— only that it did. You are all I can think about. All I *want* to think about. I wake up with you on my mind and fall asleep to thoughts of you. I want to hear all your secrets. Everything you like and don't like. Your fears, your dreams, and all of your favorite memories."

With her hand in mine, I moved it so our fingers were entwined. With my free hand, I cupped her cheek and looked straight into her gorgeous blue eyes as I continued. "But mostly, I want to be with you, at your side while you make new memories. You can scratch and hiss, Brittany. But I'm going to hold you tight and love you, because I no longer know how not to."

Her eyes filled with tears, and I waited.

Slowly, she nodded her head. "Okay."

"Okay?"

"Okay." She nodded faster. "Because I'm in love with you, too."

"You are?"

"Well, I've never felt like this before, and it's making me all crazy inside." She laughed as tears slipped from her eyes. "There's so much that's happened, so much that I know now about myself that I didn't know before, and I'm pretty sure I haven't fully processed any of it yet. But, I finally believe that I can have love, and not only that, I *want* it. And I deserve it."

I used my thumb to wipe a tear away.

"I want it with you, Trent."

"You have it, baby." I pressed my lips to hers, tasting her

salty tears in her kiss. "Even if I didn't fully understand it myself, you've had my love from the very first moment I laid eyes on you. The rest of it, we'll figure out."

I kissed her again until I felt the tension slip from her body and she melted into me.

When she finally pulled away, her tears were dry but there was a question in her eyes. "What did you mean, *I can scratch and hiss*?"

"You're my wild little kitten, obviously." I laughed and kissed her forehead. "Now, come. Let me pet you."

Chapter Sixteen

WE STILL HAD SO much to talk about. So many questions that needed answers, so many things I needed to know, that he needed to know.

But I didn't care, because, at that moment, the thing I needed most was his mouth on mine and his hands on my body. It was inexplicable, but I didn't care. I knew in my heart how I felt about this man, and to hear him say those same words that I'd been feeling...well, there was no way to explain it. Except for love.

And maybe, love didn't need an explanation. Maybe I'd just spent way too long trying to find answers to questions that weren't there. Or maybe I'd spent my whole life working so hard that there was no room to think about anything else. Because, after all, if I'd let myself believe in love, it would only lead to heartache, just as it always had.

I'd been wrong.

My mother had been wrong.

I'd missed so much. Too much. But I was done missing out.

And if I got hurt in the process, I knew I'd survive that, too.

But getting hurt was the furthest thing from my mind as

Trent's fingers slowly undid each button of my blouse, before slipping the silk from my shoulders. He took half a step back, his eyes filling with admiration, and something else—love—as he took in my body.

"You are so incredibly gorgeous, Brittany." His hands found the clasp of my bra, deftly undoing it. The garment fell to the floor.

I shimmied out of my pants and panties and stood naked in front of him.

Never had I felt so fully exposed, but it went way beyond the physical. And for the first time in my life, I didn't try to cover up or hide from it. I welcomed it.

But it was his turn.

I moved just as slowly as he had, wanting to take my time with this moment to make it last. First, I pulled his shirt off and over his head, followed by his jeans, until he, too, was fully exposed before me.

"You are gorgeous."

He laughed and reached for me.

We kissed long and slow, our bodies pressed up against each other, skin to skin, for the longest time. There was no rush, no urgency despite his need pressing into my belly.

I'm not sure how long had passed before our hands started to move, exploring each other in a new way. Yes, we had touched and kissed and explored before, but not like this. This was different.

Somehow we made our way to the bed, where we laid side by side, still kissing and exploring, now with our mouths and tongues along with our fingers. Finally, when Trent pressed me onto my back and climbed on top of me, my body was beyond ready for him. My whole body shook with the expectation of him filling me.

He moved to leave the bed in search of a condom.

I stopped him with a hand on his arm. "No," I said. "I'm on the Pill and…" I swallowed hard. "I want to feel you."

The search abandoned, Trent returned to me. His arms framed me in as he hovered above me, looking down. "Brittany? You're sure?"

I reached up and cupped his cheek. The scruff of his stubble scratched as I brushed my thumb over it. "I've never been so sure of anything."

He didn't need to be convinced. His mouth met mine in another kiss. This one more insistent and demanding than the last. Our tongues were tangled together, when he finally, mercifully entered me.

I gasped, but his kiss swallowed it before he pulled back just a little to look in my eyes while we started to move together.

He held me tight, our faces only inches apart.

We'd had all kinds of amazing sex, but nothing like this. It was beyond anything I'd ever experienced before and I never wanted it to end.

Every movement felt exquisite, each move sending shots of fire throughout my body, and eventually, I felt the familiar tightening deep inside me. "Trent, I'm going to come."

"Me, too, baby. Me, too."

He kissed me again, but right as my orgasm hit, he pulled back and looked directly into my eyes as I completely fell apart around him.

A tear slipped down Brittany's cheek, and I leaned forward quickly to kiss it away.

I was still on top of her, my cock still hard inside her, despite the body-shattering orgasm I'd just had. I was reluctant to move at all, but seeing the tear on her cheek propelled me into action. I slipped off Brittany and shifted to the side so I could pull her close against my chest. "What's wrong, baby?"

She shook her head and pressed back into me. "Nothing."

"You're crying."

"I'm not upset..." She shifted in my arms so she faced me. "I'm...well, I've..." She giggled and dipped her head. "I can't even talk, Trent. That was...holy shit."

"Holy shit indeed." I kissed her nose. It was a massive understatement, but I couldn't think of any words to actually explain how amazing the sex had been. There wasn't anything remotely adequate.

"I've never cried after sex before," she said after a moment. "Hell, I don't cry." Brittany shook her head. "That's not true. I've actually cried more in the last few days than I have in my entire life, I think. I blame you." She poked me in the chest.

I captured her finger in my hand and put it in my mouth. "You can blame me for a lot of things, baby." I sucked. "I don't mind."

Her pupils dilated with desire, but I wasn't ready to go again. Not because I wasn't ready—I was *always* ready for Brittany—but because I wasn't ready to quit reveling in the...well, whatever it was we'd just shared.

"I'm happy to take the blame for all kinds of things," I said. "Especially if they're earth-shattering orgasms like that." My eyes closed for a moment. "And damn, that was..."

"Incredible." She snuggled closer to me. "About what we said earlier..."

"That I love you?"

She nodded but I could see the flicker of something in her eyes. Was it doubt? Second-guessing? Regret?

I wasn't going to accept any of those options. "I do, Brittany." I spoke slowly, watching her carefully with each word. "Without a doubt in my mind. And before you can object, I just want to add, there's no time limit on these things. You know that, right?"

She nodded. "I know that in my heart, but sometimes I have a hard time shutting my brain off."

I laughed.

She frowned a little, but eventually joined me in my laughter.

"That's what makes you, you, baby. But I think it's safe for both of us to go with our hearts on this one, don't you?"

There was no hesitation. Her lips formed a beautiful smile when she said, "I do."

"Oh, I like those words," I teased. But at the same time, I *did* like those words coming out of her mouth. What would it be like to be married, to Brittany? To make this crazy whirlwind official?

It would be amazing. Days of us both working in careers we loved, or new challenges, or both. And nights filled with amazing sex, her warm body curled up next to mine, and long conversations about all the things that really matter.

Fucking perfect.

"I want to enact the extension clause."

"What?"

"The extension clause on our agreement, remember?"

"I remember, but…I think we've already agreed, don't you?"

"Let's make it official," I said. "Marry me."

Brittany stiffened in my arms. "What?" She laughed, but it didn't sound as natural as the one before. "Are you serious?"

"Deadly." I shifted so I sat up in bed and could look at her properly. "This is right. You know it. I know it. Why wait? I mean, it's not like we're getting any younger." I nodded, more sure than ever. "Will you marry me, Brittany?"

For a moment, I wasn't sure what she was going to say. It was the first time in my life I'd felt so completely vulnerable.

But I didn't care. I didn't make decisions frivolously, and this was no exception. I was one hundred percent sure about what I was asking.

"You're crazy."

"About you."

She sat up and the sheet fell away, exposing her beautiful, creamy breasts. Her long blonde hair draped over her shoulders, and she looked absolutely perfect. An image I would remember forever, when she said, "Then I guess I'm just as crazy. Because my answer is yes."

I reached for her and pulled her to my lap so I could thread my hands through her hair and kiss her properly.

This felt right. More right than anything had ever felt. Brittany. Me. Together.

Yes.

"Fuck yes." My hands moved down her body, lingering for a moment on her breasts, and eventually reaching her hips where she straddled me. My cock, ready to go again, throbbed with the need to once more be inside her. To consummate this moment. My fingers dug gently into her ass, urging her up.

Brittany lifted herself and, with my hands still on her hips, I brought her down hard on my length.

I groaned. She felt so perfect. She threw her head back, and we fucked hard and fast. So different from our lovemaking earlier, but just as amazing and just as necessary.

We both came quickly, together. Brittany's body clenched around me, and she cried out as I took my own release.

Perfect.

Chapter Seventeen

WAS I BEING CRAZY?

Probably.

But I didn't care.

Trent was right. What was the point in waiting? We were both over forty. Never before had either of us met anyone who had even remotely made us even *think* about the idea of love or marriage. And now...

Well, every time I thought about Trent, there was zero doubt that I was in love with him. It's true what they say: when you know, you know.

And I knew.

One hundred percent.

So why was I nervous telling my girlfriends?

It was a question I still didn't have any answers for. I knew they'd be happy for me. They loved me. They'd proved that over and over and over again. They were the family I chose.

Along with Trent.

Just thinking of Trent as my family filled me with a warmth I'd never known.

I was well aware that many people thought of me as the Ice

Queen. It had never bothered me, but now, for the first time, I could understand it. I'd always been cold on the inside. In a way you can't even understand until you've been warm.

And now I was.

Trent warmed me in ways I'd been missing my whole life.

I laughed out loud at myself and how *romantic* I'd become in such a short time. It had been three days since I'd found him in my apartment with my cat, waiting for me. Three days since we'd declared our love for each other, and three days since everything had changed. For the better.

Apparently, all it took was the love of a good man, and maybe the rediscovery of myself. It had taken decades, but I'd finally come back to myself with painting. Every time I picked up the brush, it felt a little bit better and more natural.

I had a long way to go before anything I painted was any good, but that didn't matter. Because it felt good in my bones. Another piece of the puzzle clicked into place. And I knew my girlfriends would all see that, too.

"There's nothing to be nervous about, baby." Trent kissed me on the cheek and walked past me into the kitchen.

I'd been sitting on a barstool, staring into space for the last few minutes while Sheldon, who seemed to think he was always allowed on the counter now, after Trent's stunt a few days before, walked back and forth past me, his tail tickling my nose. I was just as guilty of enabling the cat, and I'm sure I would regret it later, but for now, I let Sheldon get away with it.

"I know." I shook my head. "And I know this sounds silly, but I'm not nervous about their reaction, just telling them."

"You're right." Trent grabbed a bottle of water from the fridge and looked at me, a smile on his face. "It does seem silly. I thought you would want to shout this from the rooftops."

I tilted my head and raised an eyebrow.

He laughed. "You're not really the *shout it from the rooftop* type."

I shook my head. "Not so much."

"Still, what's going on?" He leaned over the counter and twisted his fingers through mine.

"Okay," I said. "This is the silly part, but...as soon as I tell people, then it's not our secret anymore and...well, I kind of like that it's just ours."

"That's not silly."

"It's not?"

He shook his head and held my hand tight. "Not at all. These things do tend to take on a life of their own."

"These *things*? You mean, weddings?"

Trent nodded.

"You think my friends are going to want to help plan a big fancy wedding?"

He burst out laughing. "Don't you?"

Of course they were. I knew my friends, and I knew the moment I told them that Trent and I were not only deeply in love with each other, but we'd decided to get married, they'd have a list of venues, flower choices, and dress ideas. "But even if they do," I said. "I don't think I want the whole big wedding thing." I'd been a little nervous to tell him that because from the moment we'd decided to get married, Trent had been so excited about the idea. But the more I thought about it, the more I knew I didn't want a big production.

"What do you want?"

"I want to marry you."

His smile lit up his handsome face, and my stomach fluttered the way it always did. "Good. Because I want to marry you."

"Even though we're moving ridiculously fast?"

"*Especially* because we're moving ridiculously fast." His grin widened. "But seriously, Brittany. What *do* you want? We'll do it. I don't care if we elope or get married wearing only burlap sacks..." His eyebrows wiggled up and down. "Or we can have a thousand people bear witness," Trent continued. "I don't care about any of that. I only care that you are my wife." He chuckled a little and shook his head. "It's so funny," he said. "I never even considered getting married before you and literally now it's the only thing I can think of."

It was the same for me. I'd spent my whole life fiercely independent. And now, I couldn't wait to be his wife and have him as my husband.

"I want it to be really small," I said. "Intimate. Just close friends." Neither of us had any family, so it made sense. "Just the girls, and of course Shane and Phillip and…I'm sorry, I was so distracted that night, your friend with the ranch…"

"Dylan…we're not as close, but…"

"Right." I nodded. "Him, too, if you like. And if there's anyone—"

"There's only one other. An old friend. But that's it."

I nodded. "Small."

"Small," he agreed. "In fact…" He stood and rubbed his hands together. "I have a great idea. When is your lunch with the girls?"

Chapter Eighteen

THE LAST TWENTY-FOUR hours had been a whirlwind of the best kind.

Trent's idea had been insane, but also, perfect.

Besides, when you were planning a simple wedding for only ten people—Trent's childhood friend, who was important to him as well, rounded the number out nicely—it didn't take a whole lot of planning.

The hardest part about it all was keeping quiet, but it was also the exciting part.

At least, up until now.

I made sure I was the first to arrive for lunch at the club, but Sandy, Jessie, and Darla all arrived shortly after I sat down. "You're here first again," Abby said with a faux look of surprise. "This leave of absence must be good for you. I can't remember the last time you were early for our dates, let alone twice in a row."

"A lot of things are good for me," I said with a little smile.

"You look great, Britt," Sandy said as she sat next to me. "Really rested and just…"

"Happy," Darla finished for her. "Your aura is glowing."

"My aura?"

"Don't argue with me," Darla warned. "It's the most beautiful pink color. It's almost as if you're in—"

"Oh look, Abby's here." I jumped up to greet our fifth before Darla could unintentionally spill my secret. I gave her a kiss on the cheek. "It's good to see you."

Abby gave me a strange look as she, too, sat down.

"She's being strange," Sandy said to Abby. "Isn't she?"

"Totally."

"What?" I held up my hands. "I'm not being strange. I'm just really glad to see you girls. A lot has happened and...well, I just wanted to thank you all for being there for me last week when I was having my little..."

"Breakdown?"

"Awakening?"

"Breakthrough?"

"Revelation?"

I looked at each of them in turn and laughed. "All of the above?"

They all laughed, and the waitress came by as planned with a bottle of champagne and five glasses.

"Oh." Sandy held her hand up to protest. "I'll get a—"

"Please," I interrupted. "I know you all have your favorites, but if you would indulge me for a quick minute first, I have a toast I'd like to make and a little bit of news I'd like to share."

That got everyone's attention.

"News?" Abby gave me a sidelong glance. "What kind of news?"

"We already heard about your leave of absence," Darla said.

I glanced at Jessie, who shrugged. "I didn't think it was a secret."

"It wasn't," I said. "But no. That's not the news."

I waited until the waitress had poured us each a glass of champagne. When she retreated, I spoke. "You four are my family, and I know I probably haven't been the easiest person to love all these years, but I wanted you all to know that it's because of all four of you and your love and support of me that I am where I am today."

Sandy wiped a tear off her cheek. Jessie looked like she was about to cry.

It was Abby who pushed. "And where are you now?"

I didn't hesitate. "I'm in love."

Their reactions were all as different as they were.

Sandy sobbed and dropped her head into her hands.

Jessie shrieked.

Abby nodded and danced in her chair a little.

And, Darla shouted, "I *knew* it! I could see it in your aura."

"You're in love, Brittany?" Sandy reached for my hand. "With Trent?"

"Of course with Trent." I couldn't keep the smile off my face. "And I know you might be thinking that it's all really fast and—"

"Nonsense," Jessie interrupted me. "If anyone understands how this all works, it's us. I mean, Shane and I were the same way."

"And Phillip and me, too," Abby added.

I looked to Darla.

"Girl," she said. "You don't have to convince me. Your entire spirit is glowing and that kind of energy cannot be faked. I may not be a big believer in love for myself. But for you, I see how real it is."

Sandy still had tears on her cheeks, which I took to be a good sign, so I lifted my glass. "I'd like to propose a toast," I said. "To friends who are family. To being in love, and…to getting married."

Everyone clinked their glasses, and I was already sipping my champagne before my words registered with the girls.

"What?"

"Married?"

"No way."

"When?"

That was the question I was waiting for. I took another sip of my bubbles and raised my glass again. "Right now."

"This is pretty incredible, man." Shane patted me on the back and handed me a glass of whiskey. "I actually love how you guys are doing this. The girls are probably losing their minds out there right now." He gestured to the door that led to the restaurant and laughed.

"If they aren't yet, they will be soon," I said.

"No shit," Phillip said. "Abby will be losing it. A surprise wedding?" He chuckled. "And Brittany? No one saw that coming."

"Least of all me." I raised my glass and took a sip.

"Funny how it sneaks up on you," Shane said. "What about you, Dylan? Are you next?"

The rancher shook his head. "Been there, done that. Horses are easier."

I didn't know Dylan as well as the others did, but I wasn't blind. I'd seen the way Sandy had looked at him a few weeks ago at Shane and Jessie's dinner party. Maybe there was something there that he didn't even know yet. Not that I was going to be the one to tell him. One thing I knew for sure was these things needed to be sorted out on their own.

My gaze went to the clock on the wall. Brittany and I had worked out a tentative timeline. The champagne should be arriving at their table soon. Which meant things were really about to get crazy.

And Blaze wasn't here yet.

When the wedding plans were decided, I was completely on board with keeping it super small and intimate. There was only one other person I wanted there. Blaze Barron and I had been friends in grade school, and we'd always remained close.

As close as two men could be when their lives took them in different directions. Especially when one of those directions was fame and superstardom. Blaze had been *discovered* almost immediately after graduation. It was the Calgary Stampede, which was basically a week-long giant fair combined with a rodeo, combined with a whole lot of citywide parties. Blaze had jumped up on stage at the Nashville North tent during a karaoke competition. And although his singing was terrible, apparently his *look* was just right. There'd been a talent agent in the crowd who'd been interested. He signed a contract the next day and by the end of the week, he was in LA going on his first auditions.

The following year, after a few smaller roles, Blaze Barron was the breakout star in the summer blockbuster, Hollywood's next heartthrob, and…a superstar.

But through all of that, we'd stayed close. I was there to bring Blaze back down to earth when he started to forget where he'd come from. And when I made my first million on a big property acquisition deal, it was Blaze who was the first to celebrate and welcome me to the millionaires club. Since then, through some smart investing, some excellent deals on my end, and some prime movie roles for Blaze, we'd both earned ourselves a seat in the billionaires club. But through it all, we'd been there for each other. Always.

Which was why I did not want to get married without him there.

But if he didn't show up soon, I would. Brittany was my first priority. My only priority.

"So, no cold feet?" Phillip crossed the room to stand with me.

"Not at all," I told him confidently. "Maybe that's the gift of maturity and experience. I know exactly what I want. And there are no doubts in my mind that Brittany is exactly what I want. For the rest of our lives. I'm almost positive I wouldn't have been able to say that twenty years ago." I chuckled, because there was no way I would have said that twenty years ago. "I've lived my whole life going after what I want and not second-guessing my decisions," I continued. "I'm not about to do that now."

Phillip raised his glass to me. "I get it, man. One hundred percent. When you know, you know."

"What do we know?" The door burst open and Blaze, always one to make an entrance, arrived.

"You're late." I crossed the room and gave my buddy a hug. "But that's nothing new."

Blaze pretended to be offended. "I am right on time." He turned to Phillip. "Hey there. I'm Blaze. Nice to meet you."

"Phillip." They shook hands before I introduced him to both Shane and Dylan as well. None of the guys made a big deal about Blaze's celebrity, including Blaze, which was one of the things I appreciated about him. He might be one of the hottest and most recognizable celebrities in the world, but he was still just my buddy.

"Now that you're here…" I looked at the clock again, right as a shriek came from the other room. "I'd say Brittany just told them the news."

"It's almost time, then," Shane said.

Blaze tilted his head. "What's almost time? What news?"

"He didn't tell you why you were coming?" Dylan asked.

Blaze shook his head. "He just said he needed me. So here I am."

"Damn, that's friendship." Dylan nodded his head in appreciation.

"It sure is." I looked at the group of guys. "And I'd do the same for any of you." I turned to Blaze. "I'm getting married today," I told him simply. "I couldn't do that without you here, too."

"Married?"

I nodded with a grin.

"Fuck, man." He looked down and shook his head. For a moment, I thought he might tell me I was making a mistake, or suggest he start the car so we could take off and get out of there. Instead, he looked up with his trademarked bright smile. "That's friggin' awesome, Trent." He pulled me in for another hug and slapped my back. "I never thought I'd see this day. She must be pretty amazing."

"She's phenomenal."

Over Blaze's shoulder, I noticed the manager of the club had popped his head into our room and made eye contact. He nodded.

Good. My little surprise was in place.

It was time.

I'd never been the type of little girl to dream about my wedding. I'd never had any pictures in my head of white, flowing gowns, or tall, tiered cakes. Not one time had I imagined dancing to "our song" with my new husband in his fancy tux.

Years earlier when Abby, Sandy, and Jessie had all married their first husbands, I'd played the role of dutiful bridesmaid. I'd thrown parties, worn peach, yellow, and baby-blue dresses the way I was asked. But despite doing my best to be a good friend and supporter of the brides-to-be, I'd never one time felt envious in any way. In fact, it was always quite the opposite.

Every time I walked down the aisle at one of my friends' weddings, carrying my matching bouquet, stepping just right to the rhythm of the music, I hadn't felt anything at all.

But this was different in every single way.

I'd chosen a very simple white dress. It was ivory. Fitted over my curves and cut low down my back. Elegant and simple. I wore my hair down, a bedazzled barrette pinning it up off my face. My makeup was simple, with the exception of my red lips.

The girls wanted to help me get dressed, but I wanted the moment to myself.

When I was completely ready, I pulled the photo I'd brought with me from my purse. It was my own parents' wedding portrait. I hadn't seen it since I was a little girl, but Fraser had found it among my mother's things and wanted me to have it.

I looked closely at the picture for signs of what was to come in their marriage.

There were none. And I knew now that despite their terrible choices, they always loved each other.

"I'm sorry you didn't feel like you could have it all," I said to the young, unsuspecting couple in the picture. "You could have been so happy if you had trusted in yourselves and your love."

I squeezed my eyes shut against the tear that threatened. But I wouldn't cry.

"We all could have been happy." I swallowed hard. "But I'm not mad at you. Not anymore. I know better now. And maybe that's because of your example, no matter how screwed up it was." I smiled a little. "I'm choosing different," I told my mom and dad. "I'm choosing to be happy. I'm choosing a full life. I'm choosing love. I'm choosing me."

I kissed the photo and propped it up on the counter next to my purse.

I picked up my bouquet of simple red roses—to match my lipstick—and without looking back, walked toward my future.

Chapter Nineteen

I TWIRLED my bride around the dance floor before dipping her dramatically.

"Damn, you're gorgeous," I said as I held her in the dip. "How did I get so lucky?"

She smiled up at me, those red lips so fucking sexy as she did so. "You charmed me with your sexual favors."

I laughed and pulled her back up into my arms. This time, instead of moving her around the dance floor, I pulled her hard against me, so there was no mistaking exactly how she was making me feel at that very moment. "I plan on charming you with sexual favors for the rest of your life, Mrs. Thomas."

"Whoa." Her smile fell and she held up a finger. "Wait a minute, I did not agree to change my name."

I couldn't help myself; I laughed harder. "You didn't? Huh. That might be a deal-breaker." She smacked me lightly on the shoulder. "You know I'm kidding. I love you just the way you are. And that includes your name. I don't want to change one single thing about you. Except..."

She stared at me. "Except what?"

"Except that I want those lips on mine."

She laughed and obliged with a kiss that made me groan.

The whole room faded away as I kissed my bride.

My bride.

Damn, I loved the sound of that.

But not nearly as much as I loved the sound Brittany made as I slipped my hand down her enticingly bare back to rest on her ass. Now *that* was a sound.

"Okay, you two. Wait until the wedding night."

Reluctantly, we pulled apart to see Florence and Roy, my surprise, dancing next to us.

"You old goat, do you really think they're waiting for the wedding night?"

Brittany's mouth fell open at Flo's suggestion. But she laughed and said, "I'm not going to lie…we may have…"

"Of course you have," Flo said with a conspiratorial wink. "You're not going to buy the goods without a little tester now, are you?"

We all laughed at that before Roy insisted on dancing with the bride.

"No funny business, Roy. She's a married woman." I gave him Brittany's hand.

"Not to worry, young man. I'm well and truly spoken for." He blew his wife a kiss and, with remarkable spryness, danced away with my wife.

"May I?" I held my arms out to Flo, who didn't hesitate to join me for a dance.

"It was really sweet of you to include us, Trent," she said after a moment. "Thank you. It means a lot."

"It means a lot to Brittany and me that you could be here. I'm glad I could surprise her with you."

"She doesn't strike me as the type of woman who gets surprised very often."

"No, she certainly isn't." I laughed. "It really does mean a lot to me that you're here," I said again. This time, my words got caught in my throat a little. "I know we haven't known each other all that long yet, but…you both have become really special to me and your advice the other day…well, I don't know how to thank you."

"You don't."

I pulled back a little so I could see her face. "I don't?"

"Of course not." She smiled. "No thanks needed, Trent. The only thing you need to do now is to love your wife every day and be happy together. That's really all there is to life. Be happy, my dear boy."

I had to swallow hard to keep my emotion in check then. "Thank you, Flo. I plan to be."

"You look absolutely stunning."

I had only barely finished my dance with Roy when Sandy caught me in a hug. Her eyes glistened with unshed tears, but the telltale tracks on her cheeks told me she'd already shed plenty.

"And so happy, Brittany." She squeezed me tighter. "I can't even remember you looking so…so happy."

I laughed. "I am, Sandy. I really am. It's such a funny thing. I don't think I ever realized how unhappy I actually was before. And it's not that I was *unhappy*; I just wasn't…well, this is different. And so much better. It's like you don't even know what you're missing until you have it."

"Or it's gone." A sadness washed over her, and instantly, I felt terrible.

"Oh, Sandy. I wasn't thinking. I'm sorry. I know you and—"

"No." She stopped me. "Don't be sorry. It's not your fault my husband died."

I'd never heard her speak so frankly about Greg's death before.

"And it wasn't my fault either," she continued. "Of course I miss him, but you know what…missing him isn't going to bring him back. And I'm starting to see now, *especially* now that you've found your person, well…I guess I'm starting to see that just because Greg died, doesn't mean I have to stop living, too. It's not too late for me, either, is it?"

I wasn't sure it was possible to smile any wider than I did. "No," I said confidently. "It's definitely not too late for you, Sandy. Not even close."

I pulled her in for another hug and whispered into her ear. "You deserve everything, my friend. *All* the love. All of it."

When I looked at her again, she was smiling too, her eyes still sparkling. But they weren't looking at me. I followed her gaze and clapped a hand over my mouth when I saw what—or I should say who—her gaze was fixed on.

Dylan, whom I hadn't had much of a chance to get to know yet, looked particularly sharp with his black cowboy hat.

"A cowboy, huh?"

"What are you talking about?" Sandy pretended to look shocked, but she wiggled her eyebrows, and I laughed.

Shifting my attention to the room, I signaled a passing waiter. "I'd like to propose a toast," I declared, catching everyone's attention. Trent joined me at my side and like magic, a waiter appeared with a tray of champagne-filled flutes.

"I thought we were the ones who were supposed to be proposing the toasts," Trent's friend Blaze said.

I knew he was a huge movie star, but it had honestly been so long since I'd seen any movies, I would have been hard-pressed to say which ones.

"I'll tell you what," I told him. "You can propose as many as you want." I lifted an eyebrow. "When I'm done."

He laughed and waved elaborately, giving me the floor.

Trent snugged his arm around my waist as I lifted my glass. "I want to thank all of you for being here today and being such good sports about our surprise wedding." There were a few hoots of appreciation. "Your support means a lot." More cheers and Trent kissed my cheek. "I never thought this day would come," I continued. "And I think my friends can all vouch for that." They nodded and laughed. "But I know now that nothing good in life comes from playing it safe or putting arbitrary rules on yourself. It took me awhile to learn that, but I'm sure glad I did, because I finally fell." I looked up at my husband, who watched me with love in his eyes.

The way he looked at me took my breath away and almost derailed me completely. Almost. I had one more thing I needed to say. "So…" I raised my glass high. "This is to just *going for it.*" I grinned and looked at Jessie, Abby, Darla, and Sandy in turn, my gaze resting on Sandy, who smiled knowingly at me.

"I'll toast to that," Jessie yelled and raised her glass before pulling Shane close.

"Oh, hell yes," Abby said as Phillip laughed and wrapped his arm around her shoulders.

I knew they knew. And as we all toasted, my wish for Sandy and Darla was that they might know it soon, too.

Epilogue

"I THINK I'm probably supposed to carry you over the threshold or something." I punched in the code for Brittany's apartment, which had become *our* apartment, and pushed the door open.

She laughed and started to walk in. "That's an old-fashioned—"

She shrieked a little, a sound that turned into a giggle—the sweetest sound—as I swept her off her feet and cradled her in my arms.

"Turns out I'm a little old-fashioned." I pulled her in closer, and she threaded her arms up around my neck.

"I like it."

"I like *you*." I kissed her deeply, loving the feel of her in my arms. I could have kissed her all day. My cock, which had been in almost a constant state of arousal all afternoon since I'd first seen her step out in that dress, had other ideas, however. "And I'd really like to get you to bed."

That wasn't entirely true. It didn't have to be a bed. It could be the couch. The hallway. The dining room table. The kitchen counter.

Hmm... I liked the sound of that.

I carried her across the threshold and kicked the door shut behind me, but I wasn't ready to put her down yet. I kissed her again before looking down the hallway toward the bedroom, and then to the kitchen and the large white marble countertop.

"Is there some kind of rule about making sweet, sweet love on our wedding night?"

Brittany's eyes widened. "You better be planning on fucking me tonight, husband."

My cock twitched in my pants. "Damn, I love it when you talk dirty. And not to worry, my lovely wife. I have full intentions of fucking you tonight."

Decision made, I moved toward the kitchen and deposited my beautiful bride on the countertop. "Have I told you what an incredibly sexy bride you are?"

"Only a half dozen times." Her red lips curled up into a sassy smile. "But you can say it again. I'm getting used to your compliments."

"You..." I moved between her legs. "Are the sexiest..." I gathered the silky fabric of her gown up in both hands, trailing my fingers up her thighs as I went. "Woman in the whole entire world." With her gown rucked up around her waist, I could see the white lacy panties she wore underneath. "Ummm." I dragged my finger up the front of her mound.

She shivered under my touch and moaned.

"Nice, but they'll have to go."

I was pleased to see there wasn't much to the scrap of panties, and they tore easily.

Brittany gasped, but her breath came faster and her breasts heaved. Braless, her nipples pebbled against the fabric.

"So. Fucking. Sexy." I traced my finger between her legs and her sensitive bud until she squirmed. My free hand cupped her breast through the dress, and I kissed her hard. She moaned into my mouth, and I was almost completely gone. There would be no slow, sweet lovemaking. Not yet.

For now, we were going back to the beginning with white-hot passion.

It only took me a moment to shed myself of my pants, releasing my hard, throbbing cock.

My hand threaded through her hair and tipped her head back.

With her arms holding her up, her tits pressed into the air, her dress rucked around her waist, and her long, smooth neck exposed, Brittany was absolute perfection.

"I can't believe you're mine," I murmured as I gripped her hips and pulled her toward me.

"And you're mine."

"Fuck yes, I am." I sank myself deep inside her, making us both groan.

Neither of us needed long. Only a few thrusts later, I felt the familiar tensing in her body as my own orgasm built and together, we took our climaxes.

"Damn, I'm a lucky man."

Brittany, regaining her senses, sat up and reached for me.

I kissed her.

"I think I'm the lucky one," she said.

"I don't disagree."

She laughed.

"I love that sound, you know?"

"My laugh?" Her hair fell over her shoulder. Her cheeks were pinked from her orgasm and at that moment she was even more beautiful than usual, if it were even possible.

"Yes," I said. "I don't think I've told you this before, but your laugh is the most amazing sound in the whole world, I think."

She ducked her head. "That's crazy."

With a finger under her chin, I lifted it until she looked at me. "No," I said. "It's not crazy, because the first time I heard it, it was me who caused it."

"Oh yeah?"

"I did." I nodded, feeling quite proud of myself. "And you know what my second favorite sound is?"

She shook her head.

"It's another sound I can get out of you."

Her eyes narrowed in suspicion, her lips still curled up in a smile.

"And I think it's time for you to make that sound for me again."

She squealed as I scooped her up from the counter and this time carried her over my shoulder into the bedroom.

I put her down on the bed and she laid backward with a laugh.

"Ohh, yes." I groaned. "I do love that sound. But…"

I shed myself of my shirt and dropped to my knees in front of her.

"Trent! Again?"

Before I began my mission to get my second favorite sound out of her, I stopped and looked into her glacier-blue eyes. "Always, my wife. Is that okay?"

"More than you know, Trent. More than you know."

I hope you enjoyed Brittany and Trent's journey to love.

And next…

It's Sandy's turn next as she finally makes the decision to *go for it* with billionaire, cowboy, Dylan. But is Sandy really ready to let loose and have a little

no-strings attached fun, or are the secrets and hurts from the past too much for her to get over? And what happens when self proclaimed playboy, Dylan starts to have real feelings?

Find out next in Finally Forever. You can read an exclusive excerpt next...

And if you want even more romance...click HERE for an exclusive FREE novella that isn't available anywhere else!

Finally Forever

It's Sandy's turn to FINALLY find her Happily Ever After in Finally Forever

No strings.
   No commitments.
   No problem.
   That was the deal.

A fling with a sexy cowboy? Sure, why not? Besides, it's not like he's a total stranger. Dylan Scott is the friend of a friend, and as a self-proclaimed player, he's perfect for me to break my five-year dry spell with. Especially since he's made it quite clear that a relationship of any kind is totally off the table. When my little holiday at his ranch is over, we are, too.

Fine by me. I'm a widowed single mom. The last thing I have time for is a brooding, self-important billionaire cowboy, even if he does make my body come alive in ways I never thought possible beyond the pages of a romance novel.

A lifetime of following the rules and being the *good girl* has left me with nothing but secrets and hidden desires that I've managed to keep from everyone.

Trust me, it's safer that way. But I was not counting on having any actual feelings for Dylan, at least none beyond the passion fueled physical. And when I do, dammit if things don't start to get complicated—fast.

And it doesn't take long for the safe—and boring—bubble I've created for my life to become anything but. And now, for the first time in my life, the only thing to do is face the truth. No matter how much it hurts.

Pre-Order Finally Forever **Today!**

Please note this excerpt is unedited/subject to change/and may contain typos

Chapter One

I would do anything for my friends. Including, it seemed, leaving my two young children in the care of their grandmother for an entire week—for the first time ever—so I could go to a farm. Okay, it wasn't a farm. Not really. It was a *dude* ranch. And despite the fact that I secretly devoured cowboy romance novels when no one was looking, and every single one of my dreams involved strong, tall cowboys in tight jeans and boots, I wasn't under any illusions that *actual* cowboys were nearly as sexy as the ones I read about late at night.

And fantasized about.

No.

Fiction was nothing like real life. Widowed at thirty-seven with two small children, I knew that for sure. Unlike the movies, there had definitely not been any sexy men waiting in the wings to sweep me off my feet and take on my small family. At least, if there was, I was still waiting almost five years later.

"You're not sleeping, are you, Sandy?" Darla nudged me in the ribs before reaching across from me to open the window. She was sandwiched in the middle of the backseat of Abby's SUV. Jessie was on the other side of her was fast asleep. Brittany was riding shotgun, surprising everyone when she didn't demand to drive. Britt liked to be in control, but ever since her completely unexpected and absolutely amazing marriage to billionaire land developer, Trent Thomas, she'd mellowed. A lot. It was actually pretty incredible to witness. And continued to take me off guard.

"Oh, that's better," Darla sighed as the fresh air rushed into the back seat. "Isn't it great to get out of the city?"

Aspen Valley, the mountain town we'd all lived our entire lives in, was hardly a city. With the world-class ski hill and multiple high-profile golf courses, it was more like the playground for the city's rich and famous. Especially with more and more company headquarters relocating there for a *love where you live* lifestyle. Still, Aspen Valley had managed to maintain its small-town feel, despite the changes and there wasn't a day that went by that I felt like I was being stifled in *a city*.

"What are you doing? It smells like doo doo." I grabbed my nose with one hand and reached for the window controls with the other.

"Doo doo?" Darla stared at me, not even bothering to hide the humour on her face. "Did you seriously just say that?"

Abby adjusted the rearview mirror to look at me. "Seriously, Sandy. You are spending way too much time with children. This week will be so good for you."

I opened my mouth to object, but she was right. I'd recently gone back to work as a second-grade teacher, and if being surrounded by seven-year-olds all day wasn't enough, I spent the majority of my free time with my girls, Isabella and Willow. Although, at eight and six years old respectively, there was no doubt that they both would have made fun of me for saying doo-doo. Even if it did smell like it.

"It stinks like shit," I said with extra emphasis on the last word. "Is that better?"

Abby laughed so hard, Jessie woke up with a start. "Why so sleepy, Jes?" Britt spun around in her seat to wiggle her eyebrows. "Your sexy, hot biker keep you up late saying goodbye last night?"

Jessie blushed but didn't bother denying it. "Probably no more so than your *husband* or Abby's sex god of a man."

I tried and failed to contain my groan. I was so jealous of my best friends and it didn't bother me to admit it. Three of my best friends in the whole world had recently hooked up with not only some of the sexiest men in the country but also some of the richest. But that wasn't why I routinely turned green with envy. Not even close. It was the fact that Abby, Brittany and Jessie were all having absolutely mind-blowing, toe-curling sex on the regular. If their reports were to be believed —and why should I doubt them—the kinds of things their men did to them and made them feel on a regular basis were like scenes directly out of the hottest of my romance novels.

And then there was Darla, who had that kind of sex *all* the time and with different men, because as she put it, "Life is way too short to choose just one."

So really, it was just me who'd been living like a nun. An increasingly sexually frustrated nun. *Was that a thing?*

"Okay, okay," I interrupted Brittany as she began to detail exactly how Trent had said goodbye to her that morning. *Morning sex?* That was definitely something out of one of my books. Real people didn't have morning sex. No way. With messed-up hair and stale breath. *Nope.*

But just because I hadn't...my eyes locked with Brittany's.

She offered me a small smile and I had to look away because I knew she felt bad for me and the last thing I wanted or needed was anyone feeling badly for me.

"You know you can have wild and crazy sex, too, Sandy?"

Jessie's voice broke me out of my thoughts. Automatically, I shook my head, but my protest held less conviction than it usually did. The truth was, my friends weren't wrong. They'd been gently but consistently leading me to this realization. I loved them for not rushing me. But Greg had been gone for over four years now and while I wasn't completely convinced that wild and crazy sex was on the table for me, or if I even wanted it, I had to admit that *some* sex, even boring and tame, would be more than welcome right now.

"Maybe they'll be some sexy cowboys at the ranch?" Abby offered. "Some *single* cowboys who are more than ready to—"

"Do not finish that sentence," I stopped her. "I beg of you."

"But isn't that what you need, Sandy?" Jessie asked, trying and failing to sound innocent. "A sexy, single cowboy ready to *mingle*." She dissolved into giggles, but I only shook my head.

"I thought we were here for a girls' trip," I said. "No men."

"None of *our* men," Brittany said. "But we didn't say anything about men in general…"

"Oh thank goodness," Darla whooped. "Because I could use a little—"

"You could always use a little…"

Darla wrapped an arm around me and squeezed. "And there's nothing wrong with that, my friend." She left a wet, sloppy kiss on my cheek.

"Seriously though," Brittany said. "This *is* a ladies' week. We've all been so busy lately, I'm really looking forward to reconnecting with you girls. And so nice of Dylan to offer us an entire cabin."

"That's right," Abby said. "There is definitely at least one very sexy cowboy at Rock Creek Ranch." She wiggled her eyebrows in the rearview mirror.

I squeezed my eyes shut at the mention of Dylan Scott. I'd only met him a few times. First at a casual dinner at Jessie and Shane's. He was tall and muscular with the kind of muscles that were made working outside with his hands. Using his body. Not that I'd noticed.

Okay. I'd noticed.

I'd noticed a lot of things about Dylan Scott. Including the fact that he looked exactly like I'd imagined every single hero in my novels to look. Never mind the way he'd made me feel all warm and tingly when he smiled at me. Or the way my body came alive when he'd shook my hand before kissing the back of it. He'd *kissed* it. It was such an old-fashioned move, but I had not been able to stop thinking about it.

Especially because it had happened only one other time. A lifetime ago. With a man who if my memory could be trusted, reminded me more than a little of Dylan Scott.

I swallowed hard and did my best to follow the conversation as we got closer to the ranch. I didn't want my friends to notice my distraction. There'd be too many questions. We'd all been friends since we were teenagers, and there wasn't much these girls didn't know about me. But there was one thing I'd managed to keep a secret from everyone for all of these years. Even my late husband hadn't known my little secret. There was a reason I fantasized about cowboys and devoured as many novels about them as I could get my hands on.

I watched from horseback as the SUV turn off the main road to begin the dusty journey on the gravel to the main lodge.

I'd promised Shane Grant that the ladies would be well taken care of. We'd already made the arrangements for them to have the nicest cabin on the property, and to have any and all of the spa treatments they wanted. Never mind their choice of activities. It had all been taken care of. There was no reason for me to actually come in from the fields to greet them. I knew my staff, and my sister, Sophie, would take good care of them.

Still.

As the day had gone on, their arrival drawing closer, I'd been drawn in like a magnet. My eyes had scanned the fields all day, looking for signs of the women. Or, more specifically, one woman in particular.

I'd only met her once. Briefly. But it was enough to know I should stay away from her.

Sandy Clark.

She wasn't my type. Not even close.

Sandy was *soft* and feminine. Her eyes held a sadness that despite her warm and friendly demeanour, she wore like a cloak. I preferred my women a little rougher around the edges. I preferred them to have an edge because those were the type of women who understood the only arrangement I would agree to.

Sex. A hard fuck in the barn or out in the field. Occasionally in the back of the truck. Never in a bed. Nothing intimate. Nothing serious. Not ever. I wasn't built for settling down. Never had been and I didn't see that changing anytime soon.

Which is why I should have done myself a favour and stayed as far away from the main lodge, and the arrival of the women—and Sandy Clark—as possible. It wouldn't even be unusual, and Sophie sure as hell wouldn't say anything if I didn't show up. As the owner of Rock Creek Ranch, I spent most of my time anywhere but the actual ranch.

That wasn't true.

I spent my time on the *real* ranch and as far away from the guests and the bullshit of the touristy bastardized version of my ranch as I possibly could. It was my sister Sophie's idea to start up a guest ranch complete with spa services and watered-down ranching activities so rich city slickers could come out to the mountains and throw their money around.

And they certainly did.

I couldn't argue with that part of the arrangement. My little sister certainly had been right. The profitability of the ranch had skyrocketed since we'd opened, not that it mattered. Rock Creek was one of the most successful ranches in the country. We not only handled a massive share of beef production for Western Canada but also for export. And before the expansion into tourism, we'd branched out into horse breeding and now Rock Creek Ranch was also known for the highest quality ranching and performance horses around. Yes, the *real* operations were thriving. But the businessman in me couldn't deny how lucrative the tourism trade had been, too.

It was the only reason I tolerated it. Plus it gave Sophie something to take charge of, and now with my two nephews helping out with the operations on that side, it meant that I really didn't have to get involved. If I didn't want to.

And I didn't.

Except for today…

My eyes followed the SUV that was finally approaching the parking area. I gave my horse, Cash a kick. "Come on," I told him. "Let's get down there."

Always ready for a run through the field, Cash crossed the distance with ease. I handed his reigns to a stable hand and with my eyes focused on the black SUV, crossed the parking lot.

It was a bad idea. I knew it was. But there were a million ways I could justify it. Besides, just because I was greeting the ladies, didn't mean a damn thing.

I reached the vehicle and the car door at the same time as my nephews, Wyatt and Tucker. I gestured that I would handle the driver's door and they quickly moved. I had to admit, they were good at their jobs, even if they did flirt a little too much with the female guests. I made a point not to know if it was anything more than flirting. I didn't want to know. As long as they were discreet, I didn't care. I didn't need trouble. Any *more* trouble.

"Ladies. Welcome." I turned on the charm as I opened the door to reveal, Phillip Conrad's woman, Abby. Brittany Donahue, the tall leggy blond, stepped from the passenger door. I'd been at her wedding to Trent. It had been a very small affair, I'd been surprised to get an invite. But not at all disappointed because it gave me a chance to see Sandy again.

My eyes went directly to the back door that Sandy was emerging from.

She had no idea how sexy she looked in her soft pink t-shirt and worn jeans. Her hair swung from side to side in a ponytail that hung down her back as she turned back to the car to help her friend, Darla out. It wasn't until Darla stood next to her that Sandy turned around and met my gaze.

She froze and despite the warm day, her nipples hardened to peaks beneath the tight fabric of her shirt.

Fuck, yes.

"Dylan!" Jessie, Shane Grant's fiance stepped between us, breaking my stare which was probably a good thing because my body had already responded to Sandy. "Thank you so much for having us." I hugged Jessie and kissed her on the cheeks.

"We are happy to have you." I tried to make eye contact with Sandy again, but with everyone milling around, it was impossible to single her out without making it obvious. "I wanted to make sure you all got here without too much trouble. Let's get you all settled."

I turned to see Wyatt and Tucker were already pulling suitcases from the back while they chatted with the other women. Wyatt was giving Sandy in particular, a little more attention than I preferred.

Older women were exactly what my young, dumb and full

of come nephews preferred, especially if it earned them a healthy tip at the end of their stay, but these women, particularly Sandy Clark, were off-limits. To *everyone*.

I cleared my throat. "My nephews Wyatt and Tucker will take your things to your cabin while we get you checked in. If you need anything, it is their job to help you out." I focused my gaze on Wyatt. "They're good *kids*," I said. "And they won't bother you."

Message received, Wyatt nodded once and swallowed hard. *Good.*

"Oh, I bet they can help us out will all kinds of things," Darla, the friend I knew the least, cooed and batted her lashes at Tucker who actually blushed from the attention.

I shook my head with a chuckle. If Tucker wanted to get involved with Darla, maybe she could teach him a thing or two, I wasn't going to bother with it. As long as they left Sandy alone.

She was *mine.*

The thought hit hard and fast and fuck me, if it didn't take my breath away.

No. She is *not* mine. I wasn't some friggin' neanderthal. This woman was way too sweet and *good* for me. Nothing good could come from anything with her.

Purposely, I avoided eye contact with her and focused on the other ladies as I waved my arm and led them toward the lobby. "Let's get you settled."

Pre-Order Finally Forever **Today!**

About the Author

Elena Aitken is a USA Today Bestselling Author of more than fifty romance and women's fiction novels. The mother of 'grown up' twins, Elena now lives with her very own mountain man in the heart of the very mountains she writes about. She can often be found with her toes in the lake and a glass of wine in her hand, dreaming up her next book and working on her own happily ever after.

To learn more about Elena:
www.elenaaitken.com
elena@elenaaitken.com